BRON
TARN

The Blades of Janus
PACK
PROGENITOR

The Forbidden Knights
FORBIDDEN INSTINCT

The Summer Park Psychics
WANDERING SOUL
WHISPERING HEARTS
LINGERING TOUCH
THE SUMMER PARK PSYCHICS OMNIBUS

Other Works
CRAFTING A WRITER'S LIFE: Building a Foundation

Coming Soon

The Blades of Janus
PERIHELION

Cygnian 7
ROM

Tarn: A Scifi Alien Warriors Romance

Cygnian 7
Book Six

Cassandra Chandler

Copyright Page

Tarn: A Scifi Alien Warriors Romance
Cygnian 7, Book Six
Copyright © 2024 by Cassandra Chandler
Print ISBN: 978-1-945702-97-6
Digital ISBN: 978-1-945702-96-9

First eBook edition: October 2024
First print edition: October 2024
10 9 8 7 6 5 4 3 2 1

cassandra-chandler.com
P.O. Box 91
Mission, Kansas 66201

Chapter One

"I had a really great time tonight." Nancy strolled along Main Street holding hands with an actual Cygnian warrior. She still couldn't believe her besties, Lian and Olivia, had set her up on a date with Rom.

Okay, she could seriously believe it. The three of them would do anything for each other. Lian and Olivia both had Cygnian soulmates of their own, so they definitely had an in with the group—especially since they were both pregnant with the first human-Cygnian children and the Cygnians were super interested in repopulating their species.

Nancy's date with Rom still seemed like a dream. Not a perfect dream, but a really pleasant one. She'd left her blonde hair down, styling it to look perfectly natural. Even though they'd gone out at night, she had kept her makeup understated, just enough to highlight her blue eyes. And she'd opted for comfort over drop-dead gorgeous, with a nice blouse and slacks. There weren't many fancy restaurants in Harbor, and she didn't want to be overdressed for the evening.

"I had a great time, too." Rom cast the most charming cock-eyed smile at her she'd ever seen. "But..."

Damn.

Nancy stopped and turned to face him. She tilted her head to one side and smiled, as if that would soften the blow from saying aloud what they both already knew.

"But..." she began. "We're not soulmates."

Rom's smile deepened, but little lines appeared around the corners of his eyes. She didn't have to have a soulmate connection with him to see that he was deeply disappointed.

"Not soulmates," he said, pulling her closer with the hand he still held. "That doesn't mean we can't have a little fun."

Nancy laughed and shook her head. "They warned me you were a lady killer."

His smile vanished. "Who says—"

"Oh, sorry," she quickly broke in. "Sorry, it's an Earth expression. It just means you're very charming."

"Oh." He seemed mildly appeased.

Nancy stepped closer, their chests almost touching. She should be feeling thrills at his proximity. Aside from the fact that he was tall, ripped, and insanely gorgeous, he was also an alien. That alone should be giving her tingles. Beyond that, Rom had a kind of down-home charm to him, with the way he spoke as well as his gestures and mannerisms. He had just the right amount of stubble on his chiseled jaw and hair that flopped around his face perfectly for sweeping back in a move that showcased his impressive biceps as well as his beautiful violet eyes.

She liked tall guys, and Rom was pushing seven feet, as were the other warriors in his prism. The seven men shared some kind of soul bond that linked them, like a mini, brotherly version of a soulmate bond. Apparently, their prism was a very rare 'full spectrum,' which meant there were seven of them, each with a different eye color that comprised a full rainbow. Their eyes glowed when they were experiencing strong emotion.

Rom's eyes, though gorgeous, were not backlit. That, plus the fact that Nancy hadn't felt so much as a shiver all night, was a sure sign that the pair were not soulmates.

She tried not to let her disappointment show. Sure, her two best friends in the whole world had bonded with Cygnian warriors in this particular prism. That didn't mean that Nancy would find her soulmate among the remaining two who hadn't bonded with Earthlings. And that didn't mean she *wouldn't* find her soulmate with some other hot Cygnian out there.

Now that the Cygnians knew their soulmates could be found on Earth—and that they could reproduce to create Cygnian children—Nancy was sure they would be coming to Earth in droves. Secret droves, so the rest of the planet didn't catch on that aliens were real and had settled in the small town of Harbor, Kansas. But droves, nonetheless.

She was certain she'd find a soulmate among them. It just would have been so much cooler if it had been among the same prism as her best friends.

Rom released her hand, but only so he could run both of his along her arms. He leaned down, eyes fixed on her lips. A fluttering feeling rose up in Nancy's stomach. Not butterflies. Not anticipation. It was closer to panic. She shifted the strap of her oversized purse, breaking out of the moment.

"Sorry," she said. "I need to check on Hazel real quick."

One of her standby tricks when she went on a date she wasn't sure about was to bring along her longhaired, brindle, teacup dachshund. It wasn't too much of a stretch —Hazel usually went everywhere with Nancy. Except for super-special dates, Nancy got a sitter. Olivia and Lian had both offered, but Nancy used their pregnancies as an excuse to keep the dog with her. In truth, she wanted to have a buffer if she needed it. Like now.

She pulled her purse around in front of her and peeked in. Hazel was asleep, as Nancy had expected, flopped on her side with her paws holding her favorite ball. The purse was custom made, with a big compartment for Hazel that had tons of ventilation and material that the doggie could see out of, but that people couldn't see through from the outside. Nancy always left the top part open, so Hazel could pop out if she needed attention.

The bottom half of the purse held a compartment filled with food, treats, a dish, a water bottle, and toys. The actual purse stuff that a normal person would use was crammed into various pockets on the outside of the purse. It was still stylish—Nancy had designed it herself—so that it was also functional, just the way she liked things to be.

Looking back at Rom... she admitted to herself he definitely had a style all his own. Nancy was certain he was functional, especially given how popular he had become around town with the ladies. Unfortunately, he just didn't do it for her. Being around him felt the same to her as being around Nuar or Bron, Lian and Olivia's soulmates.

"She doing okay?" Rom asked.

"Yeah, she's sleeping."

"I still can't believe that's a dog." Rom laughed. "It's incredible how much variety you Earthlings have created in the canine species, and all without genetic engineering."

"I'm sure Olivia has told you before, we did genetically engineer them with selective breeding. We just did it the long way."

"Right."

They both continued at the same time, quoting one of Olivia's little mini-lectures. "Thousands of years of selective breeding." They laughed, and Rom found Nancy's hands again, holding them up between them.

"I think I get what's happening here," Rom said.

"You do?"

"You thought we might be soulmates. Wanted it, even."

There was only a trace of wistfulness to his words, but no surprise. She narrowed her eyes and angled her head to the side.

"You already knew we weren't," she said.

"I mean, I hoped." He shrugged one massive blue shoulder, obviously trying to play off the importance of the topic. His eyes were pinched around the edges, his body tense, betraying a deep hurt Nancy could see within him. "But I didn't think so."

"Why is that?" She kept her tone neutral, openly curious and not judgmental. Soulmates or not, she wanted him to feel like he could talk to her.

"The others all have been on edge for months. Talking about how their spine plates kept vibrating, their moods were shifting—more than usual. Ever since we met our first Earthling, Buddy, and heard his sisters sing, the others had felt the pull to Earth. Every one of them."

"But not you," she said gently.

"Not me." Rom shrugged again. He smiled, but the lines around his eyes deepened. "I don't know if my soulmate hasn't been born yet or if she was and..." He shook his head. "Humans are fragile."

"Rom, I—" Nancy's heart ached at the sadness that laced his words. She squeezed his hands reassuringly, but he went on before she could say more.

"It's okay. Maker, I don't know why I even shared that with you. I haven't told anyone. You're just so damned easy to talk to."

"That is one of my superpowers. I can also tell when people are hurting."

He shrugged again. "I have my own ways of dealing with it. And speaking of that, I really do think we can have fun together. Except I don't think you're going to be okay with that until you're sure you don't have a soulmate in my prism."

"I don't understand."

He pulled one of her hands into the crook of his elbow and started leading her down the sidewalk again. "It's a beautiful night."

She looked up at the stars twinkling above. The summer sky was absolutely clear, the evening nice and cool for once.

"It is," she said.

"How would you like a closer look?"

Her heartbeat picked up and a huge smile crossed her face. "Wait, do you mean…"

Rom nodded toward the edge of town, beyond which was a spaceport disguised as a small airport. The Cygnians had a hangar assigned to them, though their main ship had been off planet for a bit. Nancy was one of the few people who knew it was guarding some secret base where the Cygnians were studying mysterious technology they'd discovered.

"Oh my gosh, come on!" Nancy gave a little skip, then started pulling Rom faster toward the edge of the buildings.

Harbor was not a big town, and they reached the last building in no time. Instead of heading to the spaceport, Rom led her down a path that curved into a woodland trail. Nancy followed along, knowing that she could trust him. The Cygnians were incredibly honorable, and they revered women. It was yet another reason she wanted to find a soulmate among them so badly.

Light filtered through the trees ahead. They rounded a bend to see a beautiful, crystalline ship hovering a few feet above the ground. Nancy had seen shards, the Cygnians' personal fighters, fly around town from time to time. She'd never seen one up close. The milky-white crystal emitted its own light, easily illuminating the trees and bushes surrounding the small clearing around it. A section of the crystal began to lower, forming both a hatch and a ramp they could use to enter.

Nancy cast a quick, questioning smile at Rom. He nodded, releasing her arm. She ran forward, first looking all around the outside of the ship. It was really small— much smaller than the shuttles most of the aliens living in Harbor used. But it was also sleek and flashy, more akin to the high-end sports cars she'd ridden in with guys she'd dated in the past. She ran her hand over the crystal surface and laughed when a wave of rainbow opalescence followed her touch.

Rom was waiting for her at the bottom of the ramp. "So, are you interested in an up close and personal view of your solar system?"

"Absolutely," Nancy said. Her cheeks hurt, she was smiling so broadly. Rom gestured for her to board the vessel, and she quickly did so.

The interior was more cramped than she anticipated, until she remembered that Cygnians piloted these things from a prone position. She sat cross-legged, as close to one of the sides of the shard as she could manage. Rom crawled in after her. The ramp lifted, sealing them in.

"Is this okay?" she asked, a hint of nerves entering her voice.

"It's fine," Rom said.

Rom had really hit the heart of the issue earlier. While she didn't necessarily mind the idea of something happening between them, she subconsciously wanted to be certain that the last single Cygnian, Tarn, wasn't her soulmate. It was such a longshot that he might be. From everything she'd heard, his was a quiet, guarded personality. That didn't quite seem a good match for her 'everyone is my best friend, they just don't know it yet' outlook. Still, the idea of doing anything more intimate with Rom and then finding out that one of his best friends was the guy she was meant to be with… Awkward didn't begin to cover that scenario.

The controls protruded from the front of the ship, somewhat resembling bicycle handles, but way more high-tech. Rom gripped them, and a section of the crystal wall in front of him flickered, lighting up to show them a view of the woods in front of them. Readouts that Nancy didn't understand scrolled up the monitor. She held her purse on her lap, checking Hazel again as the ship started to move. She didn't feel a thing, but the images on the monitor changed, letting her know what was happening outside.

The ship rose straight up, hovering above the trees. The angle changed as it pointed toward the stars above, then suddenly they were heading up, up, up, stars filling the field of view. She squealed, even though she didn't feel the inertia, and grabbed onto the back of Rom's shirt. He chuckled, then rolled the ship in a maneuver that had her screaming.

Hazel popped her head up out of the bag and started barking like crazy, the sharp sound echoing in the small space. Rom stabilized the ship, laughing along with Nancy as she tried to soothe the little dog.

"Sorry about that," Rom said, staring at Hazel. "I didn't mean to disturb your nap."

Hazel grumbled, then lowered herself back into the bag. Nancy laughed again, her eyes locking with Rom's as they smiled at each other. No matter what else the future held, she would remember this moment forever. And whatever happened between them, she hoped this was the beginning of a lifelong friendship.

Chapter Two

The *Arrow* had become a ghost ship. Kral, Lar, and Dorn had yet to return from helping their soulmates resettle their families in Harbor, Kansas, where they would be safe from being targeted by the Cygnians' many enemies. Nuar and Bron would be staying on Earth indefinitely, raising their families on their soulmates' homeworld—which, conveniently, was under the protection of the most technologically advanced sentients in the galaxy, the Vegans. And Rom was on a date, hopefully meeting his own soulmate.

Every other member of Tarn's prism was back on Earth, leaving him alone on the crystalline vessel. With how little he left engineering, Tarn could understand why they might think he enjoyed solitude. The reality was that he actually hated it. And Tarn was certain he was going to be alone much more in the future. He was about to be the last member of their prism not to have a soulmate of his own.

He wanted to be happy for the others. He *was* happy for them. However, prior to arriving on Earth, Tarn had been the only one who actually spoke of finding a soulmate. He had been the solitary member of their prism who held out hope that someday, he would find her. Tarn was actually desperate to find her. It seemed as if he would be the last of the warriors to do so—if he ever found her at all.

Tarn's hearts felt pinched in his chest, their out of sync beats driving his irritation higher. Rom was a pilot. He could fly off to meet Earthlings that might be his match, or enjoy the company of women who weren't. A shudder skittered down Tarn's spine. He didn't understand how Rom could share his body with anyone else, knowing that his soulmate was out there.

"Focus on the work," Tarn murmured. "I have plenty of things to figure out and fix."

He had other priorities weighing on him. They had been guarding a secret Tau Ceti base that had been built in the asteroid belt between Jupiter and Mars. Norem, the scientist behind the base, had been conducting numerous bizarre experiments there. Tarn hadn't been able to figure out the objective of most of them, even with the help of two Vegans.

The Vegans, Peri and Cyan, were focusing all their attention toward studying a trio of Tau Ceti soldiers, Tobek, Alek, and Merek, a Tau Ceti triad, who had somehow been infused with both human and Cygnian DNA, making them what Cyan called Tau-Cygnian hybrids. Tarn didn't care what Cyan did with her time, and he understood the xenobiologist's interest in studying them. Except the soldiers had also been turned into cyborgs, and that meant that Peri, the Vegan engineer, was helping with them as well.

Alek and Merek needed help adjusting to their new existence, since they had only recently emerged from their transition tanks. The third cyborg, Tobek, had been functioning fine for a long time. He had been part of the same experiment and emerged much earlier. The other two were probably not in any immediate danger. There were things going on in the base that nobody understood. The experiments and technological advancements might well prove to be ticking bombs—literally. Tarn needed Peri's help to decode them, but Peri's attention was fully engaged in helping Cyan and the cyborgs. How could Tarn do this alone?

Alone… alone… alone…

The word echoed in his mind, taunting him. He slammed his hand down on the console before him. Waves of opalescence flowed out from the site of the impact. No one was even around to feel the reverberation of his anger. Tarn pushed away from the station, pacing the length of the engineering bay. Had it always been this small? He felt cramped. Boxed in. It was as if there was too much near him, even though the bay was spacious.

Tarn's skin prickled and his claws extended. He wanted

to fight someone, but again, he was alone. There was no one even to talk to. Not that he usually wanted to converse. But there was no one for him to listen to. No one to be close to. It reminded him too much of his childhood in the High Temple back on Cygnus-Prime.

His mother had always been so busy with her duties as the Alpha Priestess. She'd expected Tarn to study the texts and join the clergy, but he had more often found himself in mechanical closets or maintenance bays, fine-tuning the technology that made their lives easier. Once again, he was stuck making everything run better while no one even realized he was there.

Energy coursed down his spine, flowing into his spine plates and making them snap up and vibrate. More flowed through his limbs, over his back and chest. He needed to get out of engineering. He needed to get off the ship. Maybe check in with Peri and the others in the base's cybernetics laboratory. Unfortunately, if Tarn left, the ship would be unmanned. He hated doing that to the *Arrow*.

He ran his hand over his face and sighed. This wasn't helping. Tarn needed to act, needed to move. The ship was big and it was empty. He headed out of engineering, jogging through the corridors attempting to get some of this irritating excess energy out of his system. His spine plates still wouldn't rest against his back.

He ran faster, weaving through the corridors and jumping up to higher levels. Something was calling to him, some need he couldn't identify. Another mystery for him to unravel. Bron had grown crystal lattices so that the Earthlings among them could climb between decks, but Tarn ignored them, leaping up the distances between decks. He kept moving. Going up, up, up, till he was at the top of the ship, where Rom's shard docked.

Rom was back, standing at the far end of the corridor. A large bag rested on the floor a few paces away from him. Tarn had been so wrapped up in his work, he hadn't even realized the shard had returned. More energy pulsed down his spine. His spine plates hummed as they vibrated intensely. His hearts felt as though they might burst any moment, his skin was suddenly electrified with energy.

Rom was bent over someone, facing away from Tarn. Had he brought the Earthling back with him? That must mean she was his soulmate. But if the woman was Rom's soulmate, why were his spine plates still flat against his back? Surely, he wouldn't have brought one of his romantic conquests all the way back to the *Arrow*.

Rom stepped aside, revealing the small Earthling standing next to him. Her hair was the same gold as Earth's sun, her large eyes as blue as the summer sky. She had delicate, rounded features and a trim build. Tarn's hearts stuttered, then began pounding frantically. He could barely breathe. His spine plates increased their vibrations, resonating through the crystal walls surrounding him strong enough to send rainbows flowing along their surfaces. She was smiling, and Tarn swore the light of her smile was brighter than the glow from the crystal walls surrounding her.

But she was smiling at Rom.

Rom, who stood close to her.

Rom, who had his hands casually resting on her shoulders.

Rom, who was *touching Tarn's soulmate.*

Tarn's mind clouded with rage. He charged down the corridor. The woman's smile vanished, her eyes wide and mouth dropping open as she stared at Tarn. Rom lunged to the side to meet Tarn's attack, moving away from the woman. Tarn launched himself into the air, pulling back his arm for his strike. He came down with all the force he could gather, slamming his fist into Rom's face. The other Cygnian staggered to the side, the blow almost taking him to his knees.

The woman screamed, but Rom waved her away, laughing. *Laughing.*

How much time had they spent together on Earth? Had Rom seen her as just another conquest?

"Hang on a minute, Tarn," Rom pleaded.

Tarn struck again, using the heel of his palm against Rom's sternum to force the wind from Rom's lungs. Rom crumpled forward, one hand going to his chest. Pressing his attack, Tarn lunged, grabbing Rom's tunic and using it to lift Rom over his head. Tarn threw Rom as hard as he could. The other Cygnian flew down the corridor, hitting the floor and skidding to a stop at the farthest wall.

"Stop," the woman yelled.

Rom was drawing himself to his feet, his violet eyes glowing with an unmistakable challenge. There was no more humor in his expression. Tarn let out a low growl, bracing his feet to meet Rom's inevitable attack.

"Oh my god, this is so not how I imagined this happening," the woman said. "You just... shoo!" She waved her hands at Rom.

"Sorry, sweetheart," Rom said. "This fight's not over yet."

"Sweetheart?" Tarn yelled. "Sweetheart?"

Just what had happened on their date?

"Please," she said, rolling her eyes. "I've got this."

"You think you can handle a Cygnian warrior who's that fired up?" Rom scoffed.

Tarn stepped between them. Rom was right about this fight not being over. Tarn would pummel Rom, proving that Tarn was the better warrior and displaying his own worth to his soulmate.

He lowered his shoulders to charge Rom again when a sudden burst of ecstasy rushed through Tarn's body, extinguishing his rage. His back arched and his knees buckled. He landed on all fours, his clawed fingertips scraping the floor, etching thin lines of rainbows in the crystal as the pleasure intensified.

His woman—his soulmate—had grabbed him by his spine plates.

Tarn turned to face her, panting with need. Her pale skin was flushed bright pink, and her own breath came in quick gasps. Her pupils were huge with desire, their bond letting her feel the exquisite torture that her touch was inflicting on him. She looked at her hand on his spine plates... and smiled.

"I'm gone," Rom said. Tarn barely heard the sound of Rom's feet hitting the deck below over the blood rushing through his ears.

The Earthling released her grip and Tarn rose, grabbing her by her waist and drawing her closer. He crushed his lips to hers in a searing kiss. His body was on fire with need for her. She let out a little moan, then wrapped her arms around his neck. Her nails scraped against his skin as she pressed herself to him, each touch conveying a desperation Tarn echoed.

Hope, desire, longing. Tarn didn't know if he was feeling his own emotions or hers. It didn't matter. They were one.

Tarn deepened the kiss, his tongue plunging into her mouth. She moaned again, welcoming him, meeting his tongue thrusts with more a dance than a battle. Her joy flowed out to him, filling his hearts. Their beats synchronized together, in time with the quick beat of her own. He sensed her need—her desire for unity with him.

Through their bond, her happiness flooded every cell in his body.

He reached between them and sliced through the fabric of her pants with his claws, careful not to nick her skin. She gasped as he pulled them away, tossing them down the corridor. His dicks were so hard. He'd never felt anything like it. He ground against her, desperate to be one with her. As quickly as he could, he undid his pants, freeing his erections, then looped a finger through the thin fabric of her panties, tearing them from her with his claws.

He lifted her from her feet and she wrapped her legs around his waist, locking her ankles behind him. Lining up his secondary dick, he placed his crown against her core, barely parting her slick flesh. She wriggled her hips against him, her fingertips pressing against his skin. He had to be careful. He should have given her his wristbands to protect her.

With every ounce of strength he had, Tarn made himself pause, breaking off the kiss and resting his forehead against her shoulder. She let out a little whimpering moan, the sound full of need. Then she reached behind him and grasped his spine plates again.

Tarn threw his head back as every nerve in his body came alive with pleasure. His body arched again, his hips thrusting forward, impaling her on his shaft. Panic fought with pleasure as she cried out, but then he felt a rhythmic pulse deep in her core where they were joined. Instinct took over. He thrust into her, hard and fast as his own release tore through his body.

She finally released his spine plates, letting him focus on the ecstasy of where they were joined. Without slowing, he pulled his secondary dick from her and buried himself deep with his primary. He couldn't look away from her, watching her face for any sign that he was hurting her. Her eyes were pinched shut, her mouth open to gasp in air. All he sensed from her was pleasure and more of the purest joy he had ever experienced. He gripped her thigh to help support her weight and braced his other arm against the wall, locking his joints into place to ensure he didn't press too close.

Then he let himself go.

Each time he sank into her, flames raced along his nerves. She was so tight and wet, her core pulling against him with every stroke. His skin was electrified, every nerve-ending on fire. A deep, pulsing pleasure spread out from where they were joined, lighting up his body, filling him with her energy, making them whole. The little noises she made encouraged him, the way she rocked her hips in time with his movements. He landed harder, thrust faster, his heartbeats quickening, until at last in an explosion of sensation, they joined as one.

Still buried deep, he held her against the wall, not knowing what to do next. He had found his soulmate. They had achieved unity. The corridor was lit with a multitude of rainbows suspended in the air all around them. The woman sagged against him, a contented smile on her face. Tarn was grateful her eyes were closed, so that she couldn't see the confusion that was undoubtedly on his face. He had joined with this woman, and he didn't even know her name.

Nuar had warned them that they needed to do certain things to get their Earthling soulmates ready for their union, emotionally and physically. Tarn had blown past all of that. They hadn't even really spoken to each other before bonding. He understood engines and machines, not relationships. Even he realized this was not the way things were supposed to progress. And now... what was he supposed to do?

Chapter Three

The corridor swirled around Nancy, her vision was flooded with rainbows. Lian and Olivia had tried to describe what unity was like, but it was so much better than Nancy had even imagined. Happiness suffused her, a seemingly impossible mix of utter contentment and exhilaration filling every cell of her body. Happiness tinged with... anxiety?

She blinked a few times, bringing the gorgeous Cygnian before her into better focus. His eyes glowed with a vibrant indigo light, his features reminding her of the male lead in her favorite Korean drama show. He was absolutely ripped, his lithe body pressed tight against hers. His dick—one of them, anyway—was still pulsing within her, sending aftershocks of pleasure radiating through her body.

The only remaining unmated Cygnians in this prism had been Rom and Tarn. Her other half was the engineer who kept to himself and never left the ship? Perfect. She was the chattiest person she knew. She could talk enough for both of them if he preferred to stay silent. This was going to be amazing. She just needed to figure out where that anxiety was coming from.

"Wow, that was—" she began.

"A mistake."

A mistake?

His cold tone cut even more than his words. There was a certainty behind his statement. He absolutely believed what he said. Nancy had wanted a Cygnian soulmate so much, had prayed to anyone out there who might be listening that she would find him, and he thought their bonding was a mistake?

Her chest felt like it was collapsing, her heart stuttering. She couldn't breathe. The anxiety ratcheted up, swallowing her happiness from a moment before and replacing it with panic. The Cygnian lowered her to her feet, the lines between his eyebrows deepening for a moment as he slid from her body and backed away. His heel brushed against the tattered remains of her pants. He ducked down and grabbed them, then turned and ran down the corridor, dropping through a gap in the floor and vanishing from view.

Nancy stood frozen in place. Her vision clouded again, but this time with tears. Was he rejecting her? Was that even possible?

Lian had said that Lar rejected his bond with Sophie at first because of some vow he'd made. Resisting their bond had actually *killed* him, but Sophie somehow managed to bring him back to life. Why would Tarn risk that? Was Nancy so repulsive to him?

Initially, all she had felt from Tarn was a fierce possessiveness, rage, lust, and now this soul-crushing fear. There was no joy at finding her. No peace nor happiness. Nothing she had expected. And here she was, standing in the middle of a corridor on a space ship with no pants or even underwear. Tarn had taken them when he'd run away from her.

"Cygnians don't run away," she shouted, emphasizing each word.

She didn't run away, and she was an Earthling. A stubborn, willful, intelligent, beautiful, smart, caring Earthling who deserved better than to be dumped right after being bonded with. She never backed down from a challenge. And heck, she wasn't about to back down from this one. She might be an Earthling, but now she knew she had a Cygnian soul. She would show Tarn exactly what that meant.

She stalked down the corridor and picked up her bag, lifting the strap over her shoulder and head to secure it across her body. Peeking inside, she saw Hazel blink up at her with bleary eyes. The little dachshund's muzzle stretched open in a huge yawn, then she rolled over and drifted back to sleep.

"I know it's late, sweetie," Nancy said. "You just rest and let mommy take care of this."

The gap at the end of the corridor that Tarn had disappeared through actually held a ladder made of the same milky-white crystal as the rest of the ship. Nancy stifled the self-conscious butterflies fluttering in her stomach. Rom had told her that he and Tarn were the only ones on the ship. Hopefully, that was true, and no one was about to get an eyeful. Cautiously, she stepped onto the ladder, then started descending through the ship.

The ladder only went down one level, but it didn't take her long to find another, then another, each one taking her lower. She could feel Tarn getting closer—or rather, herself getting closer to him. Her thoughts were racing along with her heartbeat. What would she say when she found him? What could possibly make this right? And why had he taken her pants and underwear?

That was weird. Now that a little time had passed and she was taking action, the anxiety was subsiding, being replaced by a sense of purpose. Well, yeah. She had purpose. She was going to go kick his butt. Verbally. Nancy knew she could eviscerate people with her words. She didn't do it often, but it was good to know she had that weapon in her arsenal. She wished she had pants to go along with it.

Had he possibly taken her pants to fix them? That actually made a kind of sense. Tarn was an engineer. Engineers fixed things. Her stomach settled a bit at the idea that this could all be a cultural misunderstanding.

People on her own world had trouble getting along, and he was from a different planet.

"Keep an open mind, Nancy," she said, repeating her grandpa's favorite quote. "'But not so open that your brain falls out.'"

The walls around her hummed softly, faint bursts of iridescent light pulsing through their milky-white crystal. She'd lost track of how many levels she had traveled down, but now was pretty sure she was approaching the heart of the ship. Negotiating all the ladders and corridors had helped her calm down, and she was feeling almost okay when she finally caught sight of Tarn again.

He was even more gorgeous from a distance. The sleeveless white tunic he wore revealed his corded arms, the laces pulled tight to show off his trim waist and narrow hips. She loved tall, lanky guys. His short hair was so dark, it was almost black, and his blue skin had a purplish cast to it. The openings in the back of the tunic let his spine plates move freely. It was a good thing, because they were still absolutely rigid, jutting straight out from his body.

He was bent over a control console that grew out of the side of the ship, electricity flowing in golden veins through the crystal. Behind him, a huge wall of quartz or some similarly clear crystal held back waves of intensely bright light that crackled and spun in an orb of energy strong enough to make the hair on the back of her neck stand on end.

Tarn stood and turned toward her as she entered. His eyebrows rose as he stared at her, his spine plates vibrating so quickly, they put off a hum much like the sound of manic bumblebees. The anxiety she had fought back flooded through her again.

Not her anxiety, she realized. *His.*

Right. Bonding enabled them to feel each other's emotions—and they sure as heck had bonded. That confusion and fear she'd experienced right before he left must have been coming from him. But what was he so afraid of?

He had spoken of a mistake. Maybe she really had misunderstood everything. The thought was oddly calming. She tried to push some of that feeling out toward him through their bond.

"So, you must be Tarn," she said, taking a few steps closer. "I'm Nancy."

He kept staring at her with wide eyes. After a long pause, he said, "I'm Tarn."

She smiled, stifling a laugh at his adorable awkwardness. "Right."

"Right," he repeated. He seemed to recover himself somewhat and gestured to the room they were in. "This is engineering."

"Awesome. I don't suppose you can engineer me some pants?"

"I was programming the fabricator to make you some."

"Thanks."

"I didn't mean to—" He shook his head, lowering his gaze. "I should have controlled myself. I should have courted you properly."

Relief welled up within her, strong enough to bring fresh tears to her eyes. Tarn sucked in a breath and took a few steps closer, then froze again, his arms half-raised toward her. She laughed, wiping her sleeve across her face.

"That is really nice to hear." She smiled at him, giving herself a moment for her emotions to calm. He wasn't rejecting her. It really was just a misunderstanding.

She set down her bag near the wall, checking on Hazel one more time as she opened it a bit to make sure the little pup could hop out whenever she wanted. The teacup dachshund was a deep sleeper and it was way past her bedtime, which meant Nancy could focus her full attention on her new soulmate. She stood, wiping her eyes one more time.

"Maybe don't run off like that again?" She rose up on her toes, then dropped back down on her heels, shaking her head as if that could rid her of the last vestiges of the pain of his perceived rejection. "No, definitely, *definitely* never run off like that again."

"I… I hurt you," he said. "I'm so sorry. I never meant to hurt you."

"I get it. I mean, I believe you. But just so you know,

leaving was the mistake. Not anything that came before that."

"Never again. I'll never leave you again."

"I don't know if that's entirely realistic." A big part of her job was reading people, and she could already tell there were going to be some miscommunication issues between them. "We just need to be clearer with each other. I guess it would be good to sort of learn how to talk to one another."

"I'm not good at talking." Worry laced his words, evident through both their bond and his tone.

She approached him again, wishing she had worn a longer shirt. The closer she came, the more her self-consciousness faded. Other emotions lurked beneath the anxiety he was still broadcasting. Disbelief, wonder, surprise, and a hesitant joy that had her beaming. As her smile grew, so did his happiness. He stared at her as if transfixed, waves of adoration flowing from him along with a nascent love that she could feel reflected in her own heart.

Wow, this really did happen fast. But, then again, this was her soulmate. The literal other half of her soul.

Lian and Olivia had described feeling incomplete or out of place before they met their soulmates. Nancy hadn't felt that way since she was a child. She had ensured that she would always have a place by learning how to talk to anyone and everyone. Meeting Tarn wasn't like a void being filled so much as a new horizon opening up before her.

He was still standing there, his arms outstretched. She clasped his hands as soon as she was close enough. He let out a huge breath and pulled her into his arms, nuzzling her.

"You're so beautiful," he whispered against her neck. "So perfect. I can't mess this up. I can't break this."

She pulled back far enough to look into his eyes. "You won't. *We* won't."

The relief that emanated from him made her giddy. She added her own excitement, letting him feel the wonder that she felt, the incredible possibilities of their future together. His eyes widened briefly, then he bent his head and captured her lips in a searing kiss. He might not think he was good at talking, but he more than made up for it through his touch. His passion, his need, his longing for her was communicated so thoroughly, she was breathless when he paused.

He clasped her face in his hands and said, "May I?"

His desire burned across their bond, rekindling the fire within her. She smiled and nodded.

"Always," she said.

He brought his lips to hers again, more gently. His hands slid down to her backside as he lifted her from her feet. She wrapped her legs around his waist, desperate to feel him within her again. He reached down to undo his pants when a raspy, sibilant voice sounded behind them.

"Tarn, I believe we have made strides with the platform that might explain—"

Nancy twisted in Tarn's embrace so she could see the two Vegans standing within the archway. Periwinkle and Cyan froze in the entrance to the engineering bay. The tiny bipedal lizards had become a common sight in Nancy's home town of Harbor. She did not think what *they* were seeing was something they would consider 'common,' though. Their golden eyes widened till they were perfect circles, the slitted pupils within them expanding to almost fill their irises. Their emerald green scales brightened to an almost glowing lime-bright.

"Later! Later!" Peri shouted, turning and pushing Cyan toward the door.

The other Vegan resisted, her back arching and her neck stretching in an effort to allow her to continue watching Tarn and Nancy as long as possible as Peri continued with his efforts to get her to leave. He finally lifted her over his shoulder and scrambled away. Nancy could hear Cyan complaining, her voice getting fainter as they retreated.

"Peri, I'm a xenobiologist," Cyan yelled plaintively. "When will I ever have another opportunity to observe a Cygnian and an Earthling mating in the wild?"

Nancy threw her head back as peals of laughter burst from her chest. Tarn joined in, his deep laugh resonating

through her. She looked down to see him smiling at her—
the first time she had seen his smile. He was breathtaking.
The lines of strain were gone, the anxiety and fear as well.
All she felt was joy, wonder, and love—both his and her
own. She leaned in and kissed him, ready to begin their
lifetime of adventure together.

Chapter Four

After thoroughly claiming his soulmate again... and again, Tarn led her to the secret Tau Ceti base that he and his prism were guarding. More like that he and Rom were guarding, since the rest of the Cygnian warriors were on Earth with their soulmates. Now that Tarn had found his own, what would happen? Would she want him to relocate to her homeworld?

The idea of leaving the *Arrow* made his spine plates lift. He would do anything to make Nancy happy. He just hoped it didn't come to that.

"Stop that," she said, squeezing the hand that she held.

"Stop what?"

"Stop worrying. Whatever it is, we'll work it out."

"Are you always so optimistic?" He smiled at her, soothed by her words as much as the waves of confidence and joy flowing off from her.

"Yes. So, get used to it."

Her seemingly ever-present smile was brighter than Earth's sun, framed by her delicate features and surrounded by all that honey-gold hair. He wanted nothing more than to bury his fingers in its softness, lift her from her feet once more, and—

"Stop that, too." She laughed joyously. "Peri needs your help. We've already made him wait long enough."

"Peri is not going to be able to be in the same room with me for months after seeing us like that. He's not even comfortable with how affectionate Cygnians warriors are with each other."

"Well, it was super cute how he tossed Cyan over his shoulder and carried her off. Maybe you're a good influence on him."

Tarn chuckled. "Perhaps so."

"I can't believe I'm in the secret Tau Ceti base I've heard so much about."

Nancy stared around at the bronze walls of the corridor that led to the cybernetics lab and what they had taken to calling 'the death room.' No one knew what the equipment's purpose was within it. All they knew was that scores of life forms had been killed there as part of Norem's experiments. Norem had been the leader of the base when it was under Tau Ceti control.

Tarn didn't want to take her there. The thought of someone as bright and full of joy being at the site of such horrific events set his spine plates off once more. They rose and began to vibrate, resulting in a resonating hum starting up in the metallic surfaces around them. Nancy shifted so that her other hand held his, hooking her closer arm into his elbow and leaning against his side.

"You're worrying again," she said.

"I will always worry about you."

"I can take care of myself."

Though she had the soul of a Cygnian warrior, her body was so frail and delicate. Tarn had given her a pair of Cygnian wristbands and taught her how to use their shield function right away—and not just so he wouldn't have to hold back during their lovemaking. He needed her safe. Once they began to have children, her body would transform, as had Lian's and Olivia's. The modified DNA of the children they carried was somehow infusing their Earthling mothers with Cygnian traits, making them stronger and giving them at least some of the near-invulnerability that the warriors enjoyed. The women's eyes had changed to match those of their soulmate's as well, and the Earthlings were getting a blue cast to their skin.

The idea of children set Tarn's hearts racing. His stomach fluttered, as if he was standing too close to the *Arrow's* engine core. Of all the members of his prism, Tarn had felt the prospect of never having a family the most keenly. He had longed for a soulmate for as long as he could remember. Finding Nancy, starting a family with her, was beyond his wildest dreams. He would do anything to protect her, to protect their future.

He glanced over at her, thrilled at the thought of her

becoming more like him, yet not truly wanting her to change. She was perfect just as she was. But then, he knew in his hearts he would always find her perfect.

"It's not as creepy as I imagined," she said.

He had been so deep in his thoughts, he was uncertain what she was referencing. At his quizzical look, she nodded toward the corridor.

"The base," she said. "Olivia made it sound a lot more like 'Doctor Moreau chic.' Oh, that's a character from an Earth story. It's about this crazy scientist who..." Her brow furrowed as a wave of unease rippled out from her. She shook her head and let out an awkward laugh. "You know what? Forget about it. It's not a nice story."

And just like that, the cloud in her expression evaporated, along with the accompanying feelings. Tarn wished he had such a mastery of his own emotions. This Earthling shined with a clarity he could only aspire to.

"We've been here for a while now," Tarn said. "And have been trying to make the living accommodations more tolerable."

"Tolerable?" She laughed again, staring up at their surroundings more intently. "We need to raise those standards. Get some art in here. But I guess that might be problematic if there's a breach and all the air blows out. Maybe we could do some etchings on the walls themselves, if that won't hurt their structural integrity or whatever."

The practicality underlying her musings warmed his hearts. She was thinking through scenarios, the same way he did as engineer for the *Arrow*. Here was his soulmate, a match for him in all the best ways. Her face lit up suddenly, her eyes widening and a huge smile spreading across her face. His hearts beat more quickly as her excitement and joy swept through him.

But she wasn't looking at him. She was looking *past* him, at something behind him. Someone.

"Zemanni!" She released her grip on Tarn and rushed forward, gracefully letting her bag slide to the ground as she did so as not to disturb the sleeping pup inside.

Tarn turned to see Zemanni, the infamous shapeshifting Scorpiian assassin, emerge from the door to one of the secondary labs. Nancy leapt up and threw her arms around his neck, laughing. Zemanni gave a sort of pained grunt, but clasped one hand around her back, returning the embrace.

The *embrace*.

Fear and rage rose within Tarn unlike anything he'd felt before. The edges of his vision darkened as a red haze flooded his sight. His spine plates sprang up, vibrating a warning that rebounded off the metal walls as he stalked forward. His claws extended, his hands curling at his sides, ready to fight. Ready to protect what was his.

Zemanni had earned his reputation. The Makers only knew how many people he'd killed. And now, he had his arms around Nancy—Tarn's soulmate.

"What are you doing here?" she asked.

Before Zemanni could respond, Tarn was on him. He grabbed the shifter by the shoulders, tearing him away from Nancy and lifting him over his head. Tarn turned and, with a loud cry, threw Zemanni down the hall, wanting him as far away from Nancy as possible. Nancy screamed, the energy of her shock making Tarn's skin prickle. Zemanni wasn't far enough away. Tarn would toss him out an airlock or maybe drag him into the death room and watch the platform in action, up close and personal. He strode toward his enemy, determined to keep Nancy safe.

She had other ideas.

Once more, her hands clamped down on Tarn's spine plates as he strode past. Ecstasy tore through him, the flame of desire springing back to life and extinguishing his rage. She tightened her grip, taking Tarn down to his knees. He dragged his claws across the floor, digging deep furrows into the metal. Was she trying to initiate mating again? Here? Now?

No. That wasn't it at all. Though he could feel her physical desire for him, her emotions were very different. Now, *she* was the one who was enraged. And... repulsed. She shoved against Tarn, knocking him to his side, then ran away. Ran toward the assassin. As soon as she reached Zemanni, she dropped to his side, running her hands over his body gingerly.

"Oh my god, oh my god," she said. "Zemanni, are you all right? Please tell me you're all right."

"Get away from him," Tarn bellowed, pushing himself up on all fours, ready to spring forward.

"Shut up!" Nancy yelled. "You don't get to talk to me right now." She turned back to Zemanni. "Don't try to move. I'll go get Cyan."

"I'm fine." Zemanni waved an arm weakly, then tried to roll to his side. Nancy helped him, then bolstered him as he sat up.

"You are not fine," she said. "You just nearly died helping one of my best friends." Her rage grew as she glared at Tarn. "And *your* best friend, too."

Shit, she was right. Zemanni had taken Tarn's prismmate, Bron, and his soulmate, Olivia, to some secret location so that Bron's cybernetic systems could be repaired. Tarn hadn't even known that his best friend was a cyborg, let alone that he was grievously damaged. Tarn understood why Bron had kept it a secret, but still wished he had been able to help his friend. Zemanni had transported them because of his friendship with Olivia, and he had nearly been killed by their nemesis, Dean.

Dean, also known as Zakarri. Zemanni's brother.

They could be working together. It could all be a ruse to—

"Just stop it," Nancy yelled again, lifting her hands to her head briefly as another wave of rage burst out toward him. "What is wrong with you? Whatever you're thinking, whatever is making you feel those awful things, I don't want any part of it. So, find a way to fix it or you and I are going to have an even bigger problem than we already do."

His hearts stuttered and his mouth went dry. She wasn't seriously saying that she would choose this Scorpiian over Tarn? Over their bond?

She glared at him as if she could read his thoughts as clearly as his emotions. In a low, even voice that chilled Tarn to his bones, she snarled, "Try me."

She held his gaze for a moment longer, her anger softening for a moment into something so much worse. Hurt. He had hurt her again. And this time, he didn't know how to make it right.

"Let me help you." Her voice was gentler when she addressed Zemanni, gripping his arm and helping him to stand. "We should have Cyan take a look at you. Are you bleeding again?"

Zemanni shook his head. The scars around his neck and circling his forearms pulsed with a dim silver light. Nancy wasn't exaggerating when she said he'd nearly been killed. Unless it was a trick. Scorpiians were shapeshifters, and Zemanni was the best—except perhaps for his brother, Zakarri. Nancy cast a swift glare at Tarn again. His thoughts froze, his hearts stuttering.

How was he supposed to fix this? He didn't trust

Scorpiians, and for good reason. They were assassins, mercenaries, spies. There was nothing else they were known for. No sentients trusted shifters.

"I'm fine, really," Zemanni said. He awkwardly patted her hand, then extricated his arm from her grasp.

"Does Brooke know you're here?" Nancy asked. "I thought she was taking care of you."

Zemanni's lips twitched up in a smirk and his eyes became unfocused. If Tarn didn't know better, he'd say the Scorpiian looked smitten. Was that even possible?

Nancy rolled her eyes. "Very mature. You know that's not what I meant."

Zemanni's grin deepened. "And yet..."

Nancy laughed, then leaned forward as if to hug him again. He frowned and shook his head, looking back at Tarn. Nancy's smile faded and a wave of frigid anger swept through her, extinguishing the warmth that had returned to her emotions while she was talking to the Scorpiian. Lips tight, her mouth pulled into a different kind of smile. One that strangely reminded Tarn of Queen Ehmach when she was preparing for battle. Tarn's spine plates straightened further and he took a step back without thinking.

"Zemanni," she said, her voice tightly controlled. "I am a very *huggy* person and my *soulmate* is going to have to get used to that."

Zemanni cast another cautious glance at Tarn, before he

bent down to give Nancy a hug. Tarn clamped down on his muscles and locked his joints, trying to control the vibration of his spine plates, to keep himself from leaping forward again. Zemanni stepped back from the hug quickly. Nancy's smile stiffened further.

"So," she began, her voice tight with strain. "What are you doing here? You're supposed to be on Earth resting. Did you need to see Cyan again? Why didn't she come to you?"

"Nancy." Zemanni dared to reach out and clasp her arms gently. "I'm fine. Peri asked me to come and help them with a technical problem."

"Are we supposed to believe you're an engineer now?" Tarn sneered.

"Tarn." Nancy's smile was more a baring of teeth at this point. The anger emanating from her sharpened, making his skin prickle uncomfortably. "The civilized people are talking right now. If you can't be civil, you don't get to participate."

Zemanni's eyebrows rose and his lips quirked up on one side briefly. "Good luck with this one," he murmured.

"Excuse me?" Nancy said, her ire turning somewhat upon him.

Zemanni shook his head. "He has no idea what he's in for." He locked gazes with Tarn and said, "Earthlings are tricky—and this one is special."

"Zemanni…" Nancy's emotions thawed somewhat.

Tarn could feel that she was truly moved by Zemanni's words. She valued them. Valued the *Scorpiian* and their friendship. Tarn tried to suppress the misgivings stirring within himself, not wanting her to sense his unease.

"I know she's special," Tarn said, willing her to believe him, to feel his desire to work through this. Her lips pinched together when she looked over at him again, but at least he no longer felt as much anger from her.

"Then stop underestimating her," Zemanni cautioned.

Tarn bristled, his spine plates rising again. How dare he say that. Tarn had been preparing himself for finding his soulmate by learning everything he could about humans, including their strengths and limitations. He knew a great deal about humans. Beyond that, Nancy was Tarn's soulmate. *Tarn's*. He knew her better than anyone. Or at least... he would... Eventually. But he knew her soul. It was the other half of his own.

"How exactly am I underestimating her?" Tarn demanded. He winced as the cautious near-curiosity Nancy had been feeling turned back to that pointed anger.

Zemanni shrugged one shoulder. "If she thinks she can handle something, she probably can. She understands things much better than you might think—especially people."

Tarn was about to say something about that not including Scorpiians when Nancy cut him off, glaring at her soulmate as she addressed Zemanni.

"What a lovely thing for you to say, Zemanni." Each word was clipped.

"She is new to this world," Tarn warned, focusing his attention on her. "There are dangers you don't understand."

"Please," she said, crossing her arms. "Enlighten me."

Zemanni stood behind her as she turned around to be directly facing Tarn. The Scorpiian shook his head briefly. Was that concern etched on his features?

"You can't trust shifters," Tarn said. "Especially Scorpiians."

Zemanni winced, then ran his hand over his face, pressing his thumb and forefinger against the bridge of his nose. Tarn had seen Lian make a similar gesture when Nuar had done something particularly annoying or stupid. Had Zemanni actually been trying to warn Tarn? To help him? If so, to what end? There had to be something in it for the Scorpiian.

"I can trust whoever I want," Nancy said coolly. Anger flooded her tone as she continued. "What is wrong with you? He helped save Bron."

That was true, but it didn't make up for all the horrible things Tarn knew Zemanni had done. "He tried to kill Craig." The Lyrian was a favorite among many Earthlings.

Nancy flinched, but then shook her head. "And Barbara ripped him to pieces for it. Zemanni is literally reformed. He's practically an invalid."

"I wouldn't say that," Zemanni murmured.

Tarn ignored him. "He's dangerous."

"So are you," Nancy countered.

"I would never hurt you," Tarn said.

She jutted her chin at him. "Neither would Zemanni."

"He's an assassin," Tarn bellowed.

"He's my friend," she shouted back.

They stood, glaring at each other, neither backing down. The silence pressed against Tarn's ears, his skin. He wanted her to run to him, so he could wrap his arms around her and tell her he was sorry and also warn her about the dangers of trusting a shifter. There were so many things about the universe she didn't know yet. Tarn had to keep her safe.

"You two obviously have a lot going on here," Zemanni said. "Peri is waiting for me, so I'm just gonna go."

"That's okay, we're done here." Nancy's brittle smile returned.

Her words and icy tone sent a discomfiting shiver down Tarn's spine. Zemanni cast one more pitying look at Tarn, then headed for the main cybernetics lab. He was wise enough to give Tarn a wide berth as he passed. As soon as the Scorpiian had left the corridor, Tarn turned back to Nancy, wanting to make this right.

"Nancy, you have to understand," he began.

She cut him off again. "I do understand, Tarn. You

believe you're right and you believe I'm wrong."

"That's not—"

"Isn't it?" She laughed, glancing up at the ceiling with eyes that glittered with moisture. "I know that you're a Cygnian warrior and you've been out here exploring space and have seen and experienced things I can't even imagine. I know that has formed your perception of the world—the universe—and everyone in it." She shook her head, a wave of sadness rolling off from her strong enough to nearly sweep him from his feet. "But I don't judge people until I know them as an individual. I don't judge them based on my past. And I sure as hell don't judge them until I understand theirs."

"Nancy…" This time, Tarn's voice trailed off on its own. He didn't know what to say.

She let out that awkward laugh again, then walked to her bag and picked it up, slinging the strap over her shoulder. Hazel popped her head up again, letting out a little whine. Nancy rubbed the tiny dog's ears.

"I know, it's breakfast time for you," Nancy said.

"I can find you food," Tarn said, a thrill shooting through him that he might actually be able to do something for her. Anything was better than standing here, wallowing in his own pain, and worse—the pain he had caused her.

How do we get past this? How do we fix it?

"We have everything we need," she said. "Have you set me up with access so that I can palm into the safe areas of the base yet?"

"No, but I can do so."

"Good," she said. She walked past him, toward the door to the cybernetics lab. Stopping in front of it, she stared at him expectantly.

Tarn strode to her side, still unsure of how to fix what had happened between them. He struck his wristbands together to activate them, then hummed a low command note that caused the door to open. He quickly downloaded the data for Nancy's biometrics as well, providing her the access she had requested to the base.

Nancy's cheeks flushed and her lips briefly parted. The other Cygnians with soulmates had mentioned the humans' sensitivity to their humming. Perhaps Tarn could use that to help repair their bond. Things had been going so much better between them when they had lost themselves in each other's bodies.

Nancy's glare intensified as she pressed her lips together tightly.

Perhaps not.

She started forward. He knew he had to say something. To do something. This chasm between them had to be broached. Tarn reached out and placed his arm across the opening.

"My mother is the Alpha Priestess of all Cygnians," Tarn spoke from his hearts, begging Nancy to understand. "She is the final authority on the Maker and the Unmaker.

Yet I—her greatest disappointment because I was not born female and the line of priestesses will end with her—have actually encountered our goddess. I now know she is one entity, and perhaps not a god at all. I have changed my mind and gone against the teachings."

Nancy's lips parted slightly and she stared at him with wide eyes. He could sense her resistance, but she was still hearing him out. His appreciation for her grew. If he were as angry as she was, he doubted he could extend the same courtesy toward someone else.

"The teachings also tell us that Cygnians are perfect in our form," he said. "Like the crystals of our homeworld, once we have reached maturation, *we do not change*. To change is to become not-Cygnian. It is heresy of the highest order. Our queen and king worked with our enemies to alter our people's DNA in the hopes of continuing our species. I am certain that if they had asked my mother, she would have stood against them. Maybe even gathered others around her and tried to stop them. She would rather see us all die as Cygnians than survive as altered life forms."

"But... But the Maker herself altered you," Nancy said, her voice tenuous. "Olivia and Lian told me. That's how they were able to become pregnant by their Cygnian soulmates."

Tarn nodded. "And none of us have told anyone outside of our prism. No one on Cygnus-Prime knows. I'm certain that the queen will eventually accept our children as Cygnian, but my mother…"

He shook his head, his hearts squeezing painfully in his chest. Nancy's eyes dropped, as if she could see their struggle through his bones.

"If she doesn't accept our children as Cygnian," Tarn's voice hitched, "what will she think of me? Am I already something else to her? Something *other*?" He paused for a moment, collecting himself. "It is hard to accept change. Shifters…"

He pinched his lips together, fighting the words that wanted to come out, the words he had been taught since he was a child, sitting in the temple day in and day out when all he wanted to do was run and play with his friends. His only solace had been tinkering with any machines he could find nearby. Modifying environmental controls, streamlining circuitry. As long as he was improving the temple, his mother allowed it.

"Shifters are the embodiment of change," he said. He shut his eyes as he heard his mother's voice in his head, reciting the rest of the passage.

The mind follows the form. If the body is able to change to such degrees, how can you depend on their minds and hearts to be steady? Better to keep a fellow Cygnian at your back than not to know who—or even what—stands behind you.

"Everything I've ever believed in is being rewritten,"

Tarn said. "In only a matter of weeks. *I have been rewritten* by the Maker herself. And I don't know if I'm okay with that."

Nancy drew in a breath to speak, her brow furrowing and her heart beginning to harden again. Tarn quickly went on.

"But I will be," he said. "I will be, because who I am becoming is who I want to be. A soulmate to an unpredictable Earthling." She smiled at that, so he hurried on. "A protector to Earth and all those who call the Sol system home." He lowered his voice as emotion nearly overwhelmed him. "A father to our children. Please bear with me. I swear I won't let you down in the end."

Her eyes glittered and she wiped at them. She sniffed and smiled.

"That was some speech," she said.

"I meant every word." His hearts felt as if they were frozen in his chest, his lungs burning as he held his breath, waiting to see what she would say next.

"Maybe don't think of it as change at first, if that word is triggering for you," she said. "Crystals do change. They grow. And as long as you're willing to embrace that—as long as you're willing to grow..." She nodded, her smile deepening. Then she reached down and grasped his hand. "Come on. Our friends might need our help."

He followed her gratefully into the next room.

Chapter Five

Nancy replayed Tarn's words as she led him into an opulently-furnished office. A large, ornately-carved wooden desk sat in the middle of a sea of plush carpet. Paintings hung on the walls that looked to be created by Earth artists. Maybe even famous Earth artists. It was all so out of place on an evil secret space base.

No, not evil. Used for evil purposes.

She doubted everyone living at the base had been evil. Actually, she knew that for a fact. Tobek had been stationed here, and he was a sweetie. A cybernetically enhanced, genetically engineered sweetie, but anyone could see how good his heart was if they paid the least bit of attention to him.

She wondered what Tarn thought of everything that had been done to Tobek. Tarn had been altered by his goddess and only tweaked so that he could father children with her. The thought sent a bloom of warmth flowing through her belly. It quickly chilled as she thought of what had been done to Tobek.

He had had his DNA rewritten on a much more

fundamental level and through absolutely barbaric means. Lian said that Nuar and the rest of the prism considered the three cyborgs they had found on the base to be Cygnian warriors now. They really were trying to include as many people as they could among their number. It made sense, with their population dwindling. Nancy hadn't realized how much of an issue it might cause for them back home. She didn't know if any of the Earthling soulmates were aware of it.

They were talking about their people's survival. The Cygnians would go extinct in only a few more generations as things currently stood. She hoped that Tarn's mother would see reason and accept how things were. Heck, their Maker herself was okay with the Cygnians making changes to themselves—the Alpha Priestess should get on board. Nancy started thinking through conversations with her future mother-in-law, picking out arguments that might help open her mind the way Tarn was trying to open his.

Her cheeks prickled with heat and her heart raced as she thought of what he had said in the hall. Everything he had said. She still couldn't believe that her soulmate—the other half of *her* soul—was capable of hating someone just because of what they were. And she had definitely felt hate from him directed toward Zemanni. It had been tinged with fear and protectiveness, but from what she had sensed, Tarn had a long journey ahead of him if they were ever truly to work out as a couple. The thought of it was daunting, but she would be there at his side as long as he remained willing to work on it.

She took a deep breath and blew it out through pursed lips, then stiffened her spine and plastered on a dazzling smile as Tarn led her through an open doorway. Her eyes widened when she looked around her. Three circular platforms took up the center of the long, narrow room—each with high-tech apparatuses jutting up from them like sci-fi trees. More equipment hung from the ceiling above. Wires and tubes dangled down from them.

Nancy's stomach clenched. This must be the tank room —where Norem, the previous leader of the base, had conducted horrific experiments on his soldiers. On Tobek.

Norem was absolutely evil. Not because of what he was, but because of his actions. The back of her throat burned as bile rose, remembering what her best friends, Olivia and Lian, had told her about this place.

Tobek was in the room, along with Zemanni, Peri, and Cyan. They were huddled together at one of the counters that ran the length of the room along its far wall. Monitors and control panels covered the wall itself, leaving the counter as a workspace. Little gadgets covered most of it, the silvery sheen to the metal of the devices making her wonder if they were Vegan in origin.

It was weird how each alien seemed to have their own preferred material. The Tau Ceti had some kind of bronze metal they used in everything, and Vegans used a shiny chrome that could somehow reshape itself, a little like the quicksilver material infused in Scorpiian vessels. Of course, Cygnians used crystal.

A little shiver trailed along her spine as she thought of the gorgeous crystal ship, the *Arrow*, that Tarn and his prism travelled in. It was the coolest ship she'd ever seen. She loved that their technology was beautiful as well as functional. Maybe when things had quieted down between them, she would tell Tarn that. It would be nice to have a conversation with her soulmate that wasn't so... charged.

Her heart ached. She wanted to rub the spot, but didn't let herself. She risked a quick glance at Tarn and saw that he actually was rubbing the two areas of his chest which covered his own hearts. Their eyes caught, and the raw longing, the regret, and the underlying love that flowed out from him took her breath away.

He would do anything to make things up to her. *Anything* in his power. She was sure of it. But Nancy made friends with everybody. *Everybody.* Even people that Tarn might see as a threat to her. This situation was bound to come up again if Tarn didn't learn to accept that about her and to control himself. He couldn't just attack her friends.

She had loved the thought of being bonded to a Cygnian warrior and knew that they were quick to fight. She had seen them tussle amongst themselves and everyone in Harbor knew about the damage that Nuar and Craig had caused when the Cygnian and the Lyrian decided to test their strength against each other in the middle of town. Even so, she still couldn't believe that Tarn had attacked Zemanni just because he was too close to her, especially right after he'd almost died helping out their friends...

Nancy pressed her lips together tightly and turned to the group clustered around the counter. She tried to shut out the pain Tarn was broadcasting, even though it felt like her own heart was breaking. Now was not the time to be thinking about this. She just had to believe that they were going to figure this out and focus on whatever problem was at hand.

"What are we looking at?" she asked, keeping her voice light and cheerful.

Tobek stepped back, revealing a metallic rectangle about the size of a breadbox. There were bands across its surface, giving it the appearance of a puzzle box.

"Oh," she gasped. "Is this the lockbox?"

She moved closer, but stopped as a wave of panic hit her. Looking back over her shoulder, Tarn's usual dark blue-purple skin was draining to something more like lavender. His hands were clenched in fists at his side, and the air behind him was shimmering from the vibration of his spine plates. The desire to protect her came through so clearly, but an even stronger uncertainty rose around it.

Cygnians had a very different culture than what she was used to. She understood that and would do everything she could to respect it. Tarn needed to do the same for her. From what she sensed from him and from what he had said, he was trying. And if he was willing to try, maybe they could sort this all out.

"The super-dangerous lockbox that nearly killed Bron just from him touching it," Nancy said, casting a small, hopefully reassuring smile at Tarn. "I'm aware."

A wave of relief flowed out from him and his skin darkened to its usual color. His gaze flicked to Zemanni. A muscle in Tarn's jaw started to jump as he clenched his teeth together, but he didn't say or do anything.

"This is the lockbox," Peri said. "We believe we have a chance to open it."

"Really?" Was Nancy going to be present when the mysterious lockbox was finally opened? Would she be one of the first to see what was inside?

Excitement rose within her. She felt it mirrored in Tarn, though his was tinged with a great deal more apprehension. She focused on her own spirit of adventure and tried to project that toward him. Another rumbling wave of uncertainty flowed back to her, but at least he wasn't dismissing her perspective outright.

Nancy was certain they would all be fine. Two Vegans were with them, as well as a super-enhanced Tau Cygnian soldier, a Cygnian warrior, and Zemanni. She wasn't sure what Zemanni could really do, though. Olivia had tried to keep from revealing too much of how badly off he was when relating her adventures to Nancy and Lian, but Nancy could read between the lines. Plus, just looking at him, she could see he was unwell.

Cyan wasn't looking great, either. She was wringing her little green hands together as her tail thrashed back and forth behind her.

"As I have told you multiple times," she said, in her sibilant voice, "I am uncertain whether his DNA will be recognized. Touching the lockbox could trigger the trap, just as it did with Bron."

"Their DNA is similar enough that you thought Zakarri was Zemanni when you scanned him at Gwen's house," Peri said. "It should be similar enough to fool the lockbox."

Cyan made a little hissing noise, like a punctured tire letting out air. Her scales lost a bit of their color. "What if we are wrong?"

"Wait, I'm confused," Nancy said. "Who is Zakarri?"

"He's the Scorpiian whose lockbox this is," Tobek said, in his deep and gravelly voice. "The one with the only DNA that can open it safely."

"I thought this was Dean's lockbox," Nancy said.

"Dean is Zakarri," Tobek said. "He was using an Earth name to blend in—the way I used to go by Toby."

Nancy's brow furrowed. "Why didn't he choose 'Zachary' then?"

"Because he didn't want me to know it was him."

Zemanni's voice was rougher than usual.

"I thought Olivia would have explained all this to you," Cyan said.

"She told me as much as she felt she could." Nancy locked eyes with Zemanni, hoping he would understand the meaning in her gaze. "But she knew that some things weren't hers to share."

"Then you don't know…" Cyan's gaze was intense, but Nancy had no idea what the meaning was.

Everyone stayed silent, the only sound the swishing of Cyan's tail as she shifted her weight from one foot to the other. Nancy waited as long as she could stand before she prompted, "Know what?"

"That Zakarri is my brother." Zemanni stepped closer to the lockbox, his hands poised on either side.

Nancy's eyes were wide and her mouth fell open. She was so stunned, she couldn't move. Zakarri and Zemanni were brothers? Her friend was the brother of the big-bad that had caused so much pain, grief, death, and destruction. Her heart beat faster as she rethought what Tarn had said. How much of his fear was because Zemanni was a Scorpiian and how much of it was that he knew Zemanni was Zakarri's brother?

Zemanni had risked his life to save Olivia and Bron. Zakarri was responsible for the Sadirians losing the *Reckoning*, one of their last two warships.

The Coalition was doing abysmally in the war with the

Tau Centauran Assembly. More refugees came to the Sol system all the time, looking for a safe haven as they were hounded relentlessly, any home they tried to set up elsewhere being targeted and destroyed. People had died when the *Reckoning* exploded. People Nancy knew. Dorn had been maimed. Bron had been hurt.

Tears sparkled in the corners of Nancy's eyes again. The weight Zemanni was carrying must be crushing him. How could he choose between his family and his friends?

"You don't have to do this," she said, a rasp entering her own voice. "Zemanni, it's not your fault. What he did. What he's doing."

"Olivia really didn't tell you anything about it, did she?" Zemanni snorted and shook his head. "Zakarri wasn't like the rest of us. Not like what everyone thinks of when they picture a Scorpiian. He was gentle and kind. Our parents always called him 'weak of mind and body.' I don't know who augmented him and turned him into this killer. But I do know that he is the way he is today because of me. Because I left him behind. Every drop of blood on his hands is on mine. I can never wash that away."

Nancy bit her lip, struggling to hold back her tears. Cyan reached up and rested her hand gently on Zemanni's elbow.

"If things do not go as we hope, I will do everything I can for you," she said, her voice soft and low.

"Just don't tell Brooke I'm doing this." Zemanni shook

his head. "Even if I survive, she'd kill me if she found out."

Before Nancy could clear the lump in her throat to speak, he reached out and rested his hands on either side of the box.

Chapter Six

No one breathed as Zemanni grasped the lockbox. They all watched, transfixed, waiting to see what would happen. Tarn's hearts were pounding. Nancy's fear for her friend was palpable, even without their soulmate bond. Tarn could scarcely believe it, but he felt fear welling up in his own hearts—concern for this Scorpiian who was once again putting his own safety on the line to help others. It went against everything Tarn had been taught about shifters.

Unless he's tricking us…

No. Tarn shook the thought away, forcefully. This was Nancy's friend. She was Tarn's soulmate and he trusted her judgment. Even if it meant he had to reject the teachings of the Cygnian priestesses, the teachings of the Alpha Priestess herself.

Tarn's mother.

He scowled, knowing what she would say and refusing to acknowledge it. He also believed he knew what Nancy would say, and given the evidence right in front of him, he chose to believe his soulmate.

Tarn stepped closer, wanting to be able to help. His arm brushed against her shoulder. Without hesitation, she reached out and interlaced their fingers, holding tight to his hand. He didn't dare read too much into the gesture. It had been an automatic reflex, he was sure. Their souls recognized their link, even if their minds were still struggling to find a way to each other.

Long moments stretched on before the lines between the lockbox's segments suddenly darkened, then deepened, then separated entirely. The metal pulled back, layer by layer, revealing a small band of thin silver, coiled like a spring. It rested on a small protrusion rising from the bottom of the box to hold it in place. Etchings were engraved all over its surface, giving it the appearance of a snake.

Tobek looked up at Zemanni. "You okay?"

"I'm fine." The crease between Zemanni's eyebrows was more prominent as he stared intently at the silver.

"What is it?" Tarn asked.

"I have no idea." Zemanni reached into the box and picked up the metal. He turned it over in his hands.

Peri stepped forward, lifting his arms so that he could scan the item with his exosuit. "Basic elements... Trace minerals... I do not understand. It is not giving off any energy readings. Why would Zakarri go to so much trouble to protect such a thing?"

"What even is it?" Cyan echoed Tarn's question, in her

sibilant voice.

"It's jewelry." Nancy shrugged when everyone's attention turned to her. The group looked back at the coil of metal in Zemanni's hand. "Give it here."

Tarn leaned forward so that his body was partially blocking her access to the item. Her eyes narrowed and a wave of annoyance flowed out from her. It vanished as she took a deep breath and let it out, casting a tight smile at him. She squeezed his hand before releasing it.

"I will be fine." She adjusted the strap of her bag on her shoulder, then held up both hands and said, "Hand it over."

Cautiously, Zemanni set it onto her palms. He didn't let go for a moment, watching her expression intently.

"See?" she said. "I'm fine."

Zemanni released his grip and turned to face her fully, crossing his arms over his chest. Tarn stayed close, poised to spring into action at a moment's notice. From the gentle warmth emanating through Nancy's emotions, she was aware of and appreciated their attention on her, though she feigned obliviousness. She slipped the coil of metal over her hand and past the Cygnian wristband Tarn had given her, then up along her arm until it rested on her bicep. She squeezed the metal, tightening it, then released it. It stayed in place.

"It's an armband," she said.

Tarn kept staring, waiting for something to happen. He struck his own wristbands together and hummed the note that activated their scanning function. The metal seemed to be completely inert. Peri scanned it again as well, but shrugged and shook his head when he met Tarn's gaze.

"Why would Zakarri place so much value on this?" Cyan asked. "He went to such lengths to get the lockbox back."

"However, in the end, he didn't care about it at all," Tarn said. "He only cared about Queenie."

"The super-smart space kitten?" Nancy's surprise was as clear on her face as through their bond.

Tarn nodded. "Dorn told us that Zakarri approached him shortly after the *Reckoning* was destroyed and demanded that he give Queenie a good life. He said he wasn't interested in the lockbox or the Myers sisters anymore and would leave those three human soulmates alone if Dorn took care of Queenie for Zakarri."

Nancy's brow furrowed. "That doesn't sound like the cold-blooded killer that Dean—Zakarri—has been made out to be."

"He can be both," Zemanni said. "Never doubt that."

Nancy frowned. "So, if he cares that much about a kitten, he might actually love Hayley." Nancy looked down at the armband, reaching up to run her fingertips over the scales etched on the metal. "This could be a gift. Something significant between them."

"An armband of a snake?" Tarn said. "Is there some Earth meaning to that animal?"

"Not a pleasant one, in most circumstances." Tobek shrugged at Peri and Cyan. "No offense."

Peri rolled his eyes. "None taken, especially since we are not snakes but reptiles."

"It's not a snake," Nancy said, still staring at the armband. She pointed to a segment that was broader, with lines etched over the scales. "It's a dragon. See? Here are its wings."

"A dragon?" Peri said.

"Der'Eghonians are the closest thing you'd know to them," Tarn said.

Peri let out a snort of frustration. "It does not matter if it is an emblem of a Lyrian parcel. We have also gone to much trouble over something that is not as significant as we expected."

"It is significant," Cyan said.

"We understand Zakarri better now." Nancy nodded, her eyes catching Tarn's. "Hayley is more important to him than anything."

His chest felt tight, his hearts pounding as he once more tried not to read too much into her gaze. He couldn't stop the feelings of hope welling up within him. Before anyone could say more, the door to the rest area off to the side of the laboratory opened. Merek ran into the chamber.

"Cyan, Alek is having another episode," he said. "Please, he needs you."

"Of course." Cyan gently touched Peri's arm. "Will you

accompany me? His cybernetics complicate his treatment."

"Certainly," Peri said.

Peri was one of the Vegan's best engineers. He had assisted Tarn on numerous occasions and they'd been working together to try to solve the mystery of the platform in the 'death room' for as long as the Cygnians had known it existed. Peri had also 'rescued' an abandoned rover on the planet Mars, giving the robot sentience in the process. Margaret, as she was now called, was back on Earth, helping Brendan with Department of Homeworld Security matters.

"Peri," Tarn said, as one of Peri's other inventions suddenly leapt to Tarn's mind. "Do you still keep spare collars for the kittens on hand in case of emergencies?"

"Always," Peri said.

"Can I have one?"

Peri cocked his head to the side, but then Cyan hissed something urgent and pleading in their sibilant language. Peri nodded, then hastily grasped one of the rings of his exosuit that wrapped around his arm. The ring widened enough for him to remove it. He handed it to Tarn and quickly pointed out a few controls etched onto its surface, along with their explanations. The Vegans hurried to Merek, Tobek following behind them. They all disappeared into the other room.

"Alek is the Tau Cygnian cyborg whose tank

malfunctioned." Nancy's voice was low and somber. Tarn nodded. "Is he going to be okay?"

"Cyan and Peri will take care of him," Zemanni said, his own voice gentler than Tarn had ever heard it before. "If anyone can help him, they can."

Nancy hugged herself. A soft whine emanated from her bag and her eyes went wide.

"Oh my gosh, Hazel, I'm so sorry!" Nancy said. The little dog poked her nose up out of the opening at the top of the bag. Nancy reached in to pet her. "I got caught up in all the excitement. I'm such a bad mom."

"You're not a bad mom." Tarn spoke a bit too emphatically, but she only smiled at his outburst.

"I forgot about her for a moment," Nancy said. "But I'm thinking you didn't." She looked pointedly at the collar in his hand. Warmth emanated from her as strongly as when they had first met and recognized each other. Tarn basked in her approval.

"This will keep Hazel safe." Tarn stepped closer and handed the collar to Nancy. He activated his wristbands, then pressed a control on the collar that would enable it to link up with his commands, as well as Nancy's. "We've worked with Peri to enhance what the kittens' collars can do. If you activate your wristbands, then hum this note to connect with the collar, you can use the same commands I taught you to activate shielding, atmospheric generators, and environmental controls."

"Will she be able to shoot ray beams?" Nancy asked.

Tarn was confused at first, until he sensed the playfulness flowing out from Nancy. He smiled and said, "We didn't think it was a good idea to give the kittens the ability to zap people. They asked, though."

Nancy's face lit up, as bright and beautiful as a glorious sunrise. "Oh my gosh. Will I be able to talk to her? Can she talk to me if she uses this?"

Tarn shrugged. "We haven't tested it on regular Earth animals."

"But it's safe for me to use with her, right?"

"Absolutely," Tarn said.

Hazel started yipping.

"She doesn't need a high-tech collar to communicate," Zemanni said, breaking into the conversation.

"Right." Nancy laughed, then smiled down at her dog. "I will go give you your breakfast right now." She looked around and scowled. "But not here. We'll be outside, okay?"

She cast a slight smile at Tarn. He cleared his throat and nodded. "I'll come with you."

"Hold up." All the gentleness had left Zemanni's tone as he stared at Tarn. The hint of command threaded through it made Tarn's spine plates start to rise. He clamped them down to avoid upsetting Nancy again.

She still picked up on the tension between them. Arching one eyebrow, she glared at Zemanni, her own command coming clearly through her expression.

"I'll be nice," Zemanni said.

"Good." She smiled as she passed him, then rose on her tip-toes to kiss his cheek. Zemanni leaned to the side with a sigh of resignation, as if he was used to this. Tarn doubted he found it as much of a chore as he was pretending. The Scorpiian's lips twitched up in the faintest ghost of a smile. It vanished as he straightened, still staring at Tarn.

A wave of uncertainty and defiance flowed out from Nancy as she also looked at him. Tarn redoubled his efforts to stay in place. He needed to show her that he trusted her, even if he didn't trust the Scorpiian. She fixed the strap of her bag once more, then headed out of the room.

"We're not going to fight," Zemanni said, the moment the door closed behind Nancy. "I know you Cygnians enjoy that sort of thing."

"We're not going to fight. But I'm never going to trust you."

Zemanni chuckled. "Bron thought the same thing. Ask him what he thinks of me now."

Tarn would do that the moment he had a chance. "Is that why you wanted me to stay?"

"No." Zemanni was silent for a while. He opened his mouth as if to speak, then snapped it shut.

"Go ahead," Tarn said. "I promise I won't attack you

again—unless you give me reason. Say your piece."

Zemanni snorted and shook his head. "You have no idea what you're dealing with."

"I know you're an assassin. Deadly and dangero—"

"I'm not talking about me," Zemanni said. "I'm talking about Nancy."

This time, Tarn couldn't stop his spine plates from rising. "I've been studying Earthlings, preparing myself for finding my soulmate among them."

"Yeah, but you didn't just get any Earthling. You got *Nancy*."

What did that mean? Zemanni had said she was special. Of course, she was special to Tarn. But she seemed very much like the other Earthlings he had met.

"Nancy has this... energy about her," Zemanni continued. "She makes you feel important. She cares about every single life form she meets. Every one, without exception. We are all family to her. All of us. We all have worth in her eyes."

Tarn felt his throat tighten. Here was his enemy—supposedly an enemy to all sentients in the galaxy—praising Tarn's soulmate. Scorpiians were notorious for their focus on collecting resources and only caring about that one pursuit. The way Zemanni's expression softened as he spoke of Nancy, Tarn found himself believing that Zemanni's feelings for her were genuine. There was no spark of attraction, only a deep, warm affection. Tarn recalled what Bron had told him of how the Scorpiian had suffered harm helping Bron and Olivia. Tarn had been skeptical. He found his doubts fading as he listened to the other man speak.

"Do you have any idea how rare that is?" Zemanni said. "How special?"

Tarn nodded, his throat too tight to let words pass.

"There isn't enough of that in the galaxy," Zemanni went on. "You're her soulmate, so some of that has to be in you somewhere. For Nancy's happiness, as well as yours, I suggest you make the effort to find it and cultivate it."

"I will."

"I know." Zemanni cast a lopsided smirk at him. "Nancy will make you."

Tarn actually laughed. He couldn't believe he was standing with a Scorpiian, having this conversation and feeling... camaraderie. He knew it was because of Nancy's influence, even after such a brief span of time being bonded with her. It was still hard to believe.

"You're a lucky bastard," Zemanni said. "But there's a downside."

Tarn couldn't imagine there being any downside to being with Nancy. He listened intently as Zemanni went on, seeing more of the Scorpiian's value himself. Zemanni stepped closer—closer than Tarn would have dreamt he would ever let a notorious assassin stand.

"If you let anything happen to her," Zemanni said, in a voice laced with warning, "you'll have half the galaxy on your ass, including me. And 'invalid' or not, I promise you —you will never see me coming."

Tarn couldn't keep his spine plates from picking up their vibration, a singing resonance echoing through the metal walls. He wanted to attack Zemanni, to respond to the obvious challenge he was making. But Nancy wouldn't want that. Instead, Tarn said, "I would never let anything happen to her."

Zemanni smirked. "Being with an Earthling is never what you expect. They are the most curious beings I've ever encountered and have a knack for getting into trouble. Keep her close."

"I intend to."

"I don't doubt it." Zemanni's smirk deepened. "Speaking of which, I better get back to Brooke. And I happen to notice Nancy is nowhere to be seen. Better go find her."

A sharp feeling of misgiving tore through Tarn. He had left her to her own devices. She shouldn't be able to get into any chambers that were dangerous. Those were all sealed. Still, Tarn didn't like the idea of her being alone in the base. He nodded curtly at Zemanni, then hurried from the chamber.

Chapter Seven

For an evil base built by a mad scientist, the Ceres site sure was boring. Nancy glanced at the office outside of the laboratory and shuddered. Okay, maybe there was some malevolent energy still lingering. She headed out to the hallway, hoping to find a room that wasn't so... icky. Hazel was in full-on begging mode. She poked her head up and licked her lips, whining plaintively.

It wasn't like her 'I have business to take care of,' whine at least. Nancy had made sure Hazel had the opportunity to take care of that before they left Earth, and that had only been a few hours ago. Had it really only been that long?

"I know, I'm so sorry, honey. I'll get you your food right now."

Nancy started to kneel down, but then shivered again. Maybe there was a little more residual energy hanging around than she thought. She looked up and down the corridor, with its many doors leading to who-knew-what chambers. At the far end, a huge double-door stood open with a wide space beyond. That seemed more promising than hanging out in the hallway.

There was a crispness to the air as she approached, a little breeze that almost smelled like fresh wintery air. Winter was Nancy's favorite season. Taking it as a good sign, she stepped through the opening.

A huge domed ceiling rose several stories above, giving the room a spherical shape. There was a raised dais at its center, mirroring the circular shape of the room. The walls and floor gleamed as if they'd just been scrubbed and the air was definitely fresher here. She sat down with her bag next to her and lifted Hazel out.

The dachshund's whole body was wagging back and forth with her enthusiasm to be out and about. Nancy laughed as Hazel licked her chin, then looked around the room with her soft, floppy ears perked as forward as she could get them. Nancy quickly pulled out Hazel's bowl and a pouch of dog food specially formulated for Hazel. The moment it was ready, Hazel pounced on it, making quick work of the food and leaving the bowl spotless.

"Wow, you sure were hungry." Nancy laughed, then retrieved a bottle of water and opened it. She poured a generous portion into the clean bowl, then drank some herself. She set it down and shivered, wrapping her arms around herself. "It's cold in here. Are you cold?"

Hazel was hastily drinking some water, but looked up at Nancy, her head cocked to the side as water dripped from her muzzle. Little lines of frost were gathering on her whiskers.

"What on Earth…" Nancy picked Hazel up. The dachshund snuggled against her chest. "Well, we're not on Earth. Let's see what this fancy new collar can do to help you be more comfortable."

She cleared her throat, then hummed a few notes, activating her own wristbands and connecting to the collar. The metal grew slightly warm and expanded, allowing Nancy to slide it over Hazel's little face. Nancy held her breath as it tightened to a size that was snug enough not to fall off, but also a comfortable—and most importantly, safe—fit.

"So far, so good," Nancy murmured. She hummed another note, activating the environmental controls that should make a pocket of warmth around Hazel at just the right temperature for the little dog. The frost on her whiskers disappeared.

Laughing, Nancy leaned in and pressed a kiss on Hazel's forehead. She shivered, the cold still getting to her.

"I guess I should activate my own environmental controls as well." A warm blanket of energy flowed over her skin before she could hum the command. She looked up to see Tarn standing at the open doorway.

"What are you doing in here?" he asked.

"I was just feeding Hazel."

"You're not supposed to be in here." His voice was tight and harsh.

"The door was open." Nancy stood, letting Hazel hop to the ground as she did so. Anger and fear buzzed around Tarn. An unpleasant crackling sensation raced up and down her spine through their connection. "Why are you so mad?"

"Nancy, this is the death room."

"The death room. Wait, *the* death room?"

Panic bottomed out in her stomach as her heart began to pound. She glanced around, trying to find Hazel. The little dog's bronze-and-white brindled fur made her perfectly camouflaged for the room. Nancy ran forward, desperate to find her pet.

"Hazel?" she yelled. "Hazel!"

An answering yip allowed Nancy to be able to breathe again. She pressed a hand to her chest and closed her eyes for a moment, letting the relief wash through her. It vanished when she opened her eyes.

Hazel was standing right next to the platform. The platform that Olivia and Lian had told Nancy blew people up. No wonder the room was so pristine. The Cygnians and Vegans must have scoured it before starting to study the technology within.

"Good girl," Nancy said, taking a cautious step forward. "Come around the platform. Do not step on it." Her focus was riveted to Hazel, but Nancy angled her head toward Tarn. "Is that how it's activated?"

"We're not sure. Inert matter and vegetation doesn't

trigger it. We haven't dared to place something living on it since Lar witnessed the platform in action."

"Oh God," Nancy said, her throat tightening.

Hazel was staring at them, her tail wagging furiously, but her head cocked to the side as if she was thinking really hard. The little dog's eyes widened and she started barking suddenly.

"Play?" was overlaid with the bark. "Play?"

"Oh my gosh!" Nancy said. "She can talk!"

"Talk!" Hazel barked some more, a huge doggie smile on her face. She dropped the front of her body in a joyful invitation to play, and again barked. "Play!"

"No, no, no!" Nancy lowered herself a little bit, her arms outstretched. Tears clouded Nancy's eyes. "Come to mommy. Please, come to mommy."

"Play?" Hazel's bark was a little more subdued, but she stayed put.

"What's wrong?" Tarn must be feeling the utter panic that was twisting Nancy's insides.

"Her favorite game is chase."

"Chase!" Hazel barked.

"Hazel, no!" Nancy launched herself forward just as the little dog did the same, both heading *toward* the platform.

Time seemed to slow. Behind her, Tarn also sprang into action, but he was much farther away. The room was huge. He was humming something. Notes to activate shielding, atmospheric generators. Nancy saw a flash of light around Hazel and felt a blanket of energy encompass her own body. What else could she do? *What else could she do?*

Strength. She needed strength.

Nancy hummed the note that Lian had been showing off one night at the coffeeshop, using it to be able to lift tables, chairs, even a car parked on the street out front. Pushing off with every ounce of strength she had, Nancy prayed the wristbands could augment her abilities enough to let her reach Hazel in time.

Hazel's muzzle was open in a huge smile, her ears flying behind her as she leapt up onto the platform to run away from Nancy. Nothing happened. Maybe nothing would happen. Nancy couldn't take that chance. She kept running as fast as she could, each stride flinging her through the air farther than she could ever manage herself. Maybe she could grab Hazel and clear the platform entirely in one jump. It was their best shot. Nancy's feet hit the floor right at the platform's edge. She reached out, coiling her legs and launching herself toward the little dog, practically flying over the platform.

A buzzing sound rang in her ears. Nancy could barely hear her mental prayers as it became louder and louder. Her fingertips touched fur. She grabbed Hazel, lifting her off her paws and holding her tight against her chest. A second later, she felt strong hands on her sides and lurched up against an even stronger chest. Tarn brought his legs up under hers, curling her into a ball as he wrapped himself around Nancy's body, cocooning them both with Hazel at the center.

The buzzing was a deafening cacophony drowning out everything else, until it abruptly stopped in a brilliant flash of light. The noise didn't just stop—everything stopped. Nancy couldn't hear anything aside from her own breathing, her racing heartbeat. The absolute silence was like a pressure on her ears, as if they had been stuffed with cotton.

Cobalt blue light flooded her vision and was all she could see. No, not quite. She peered out from beneath Tarn's arm and saw red lights flying through the blue that surrounded them. Huge shapes with long necks and tails and enormous wings.

Dragons?

She had to be hallucinating. Maybe she had died, and this was the passage to the afterlife. Hazel was still in her arms. Tarn was still wrapped around them. That wasn't so bad, right?

Tears still stung her eyes. Tears that became blinding as they were filled with a bright, white light.

Here it is...

Her body was jarred as Tarn landed on something hard, still keeping his arms around her. His embrace was stiff and he wasn't moving.

Cygnians crystalized when they died. Their bodies

became statues. Did that mean...

Loud crackling filled her ears as he straightened—the most beautiful sound she'd ever heard. He set her on her feet gently and turned her to face him. His hands were everywhere, touching her arms, her legs, her back.

"Are you alright?" he asked. "I locked my joints so that I wouldn't crush you."

"I'm fine." Nancy laughed and sniffed, her relief that he was okay making her giddy. But something he had said ate at her. "Oh no, Hazel! I enhanced my strength to catch her. I didn't crush her, did I?" Nancy looked down to see the little dog staring up at her with huge brown eyes.

Hazel let out a little whine, and that cute voice accompanied it. "No play?"

Nancy was so relieved, she laughed, then bent to kiss the little dog's head.

"I activated her shielding when I did yours," Tarn said. "It's strong enough to protect her, even if you forget yourself."

Nancy's cheeks warmed as she remembered Tarn explaining that fact shortly after they met, when he had given her a set of Cygnian wristbands to protect her while they continued their 'bonding.'

"Nancy." Tarn brushed her hair back and cradled her face gently. "Are you alright?"

"I am." For the first time, she noticed that his black hair had turned white from ice. Each time he blinked, a sheen of frost was dislodged from his eyes. "Oh no. What about you?"

"Me?"

"You're freezing."

Tarn shook his head and smiled. "Cygnians are stronger than that."

She laughed, then reached up and stroked his cheek with one hand. "I've never been more grateful."

She threaded her free arm around his neck and pulled him closer so she could claim his lips in a kiss.

Chapter Eight

Was this real? Or were they in the realm of the Unmaker?

Lar had been to the Cygnian afterlife. This was not at all what he had described. And Nancy felt so real in Tarn's arms, beneath his lips. He grasped her hips and pulled her closer, deepening the kiss. No matter what lifetime this was, holding her like this was pure bliss.

Feeling her emotions was just as heady as her body against his. Her relief that they were alright, her affection. It was so clear in that moment, Tarn could only bask in it, his own emotions amplifying hers as their nascent bond grew stronger. Their budding love.

She loved him.

Tarn wasn't sure which relieved him more—that the spark of love was present within her or that they had somehow survived the platform.

The platform…

"No play!" An angry feminine voice cut into his own thoughts, accompanied by barking. With a low growl, Hazel repeated, "No play," a bit less aggressively.

Tarn and Nancy both laughed as they broke off the kiss.

"I guess maybe we should save that for when we don't have a chaperone," Nancy said.

"And when we figure out where we are."

Tarn finally put his attention on their surroundings. The first thing he noted was the intense cold of the environment. He could breathe, even without his atmospheric generators running. He wanted to save as much energy in his wristbands as he could. He wasn't sure how long the energy would last within Nancy's wristbands and Hazel's collar. Tarn hoped to be able to augment their functioning with his own wristbands if necessary. They needed to find a way out of this place.

Nancy and Hazel could probably breathe the air as well, but the cold would damage their lungs within seconds. They would freeze quickly if their shielding went down. Thank the Maker, Tarn had been able to activate all of the protective measures he had enabled for both Nancy and Hazel before they went through that strange void.

Now, they were standing in another spherical room containing a circular platform. Equipment littered the area, some pieces as large as a shard. None of it was technology he recognized. The room itself was identical to the one they'd just come from, except the metal forming the curved walls was a dark gray with a single red stripe wrapping around it at about waist level. Hadn't Lian described the ship that she'd been abducted on as having a similar design? But that might mean…

"Oh no," Tarn said, pulling Nancy closer and scanning the room for possible exits.

"What 'oh no?'" Nancy asked.

"I think we might be in the Centauran system."

"Centauran… As in the *Tau Centauran Assembly* Centauran system? The species who are trying to destroy every Sadirian in the galaxy?" Nancy's voice was smaller when she went on. "Sadirians who look just like me and show up on scans identically to Earthlings?"

Tarn knew his fear had to answer her question better than anything he could say. Centaurans were shifters—not quite as bad as Scorpiians, since they could only take on one different form—but still not to be trusted. They were formidable opponents in battle, ferocious when defending their territory. And Tarn and Nancy were most likely very deep within their territory.

"I won't let anything happen to you," Tarn said. "I'll protect you."

She nodded, but her own fear flowed to him through their bond. She knew he would do everything in his power to keep her safe. But would it be enough?

"It's okay," Nancy said. She sniffed, and then managed a smile. "We'll just explain what happened and…" She shook her head, staring around them at the room. Calm rose up within her, radiating out and warming him from the bitter chill. She looked back to him and her smile had deepened. "I can make friends with anybody."

How could anyone be so brave? So confident? In the face of this…

"What?" she said.

"I am the luckiest man in the universe."

She laughed, then leaned closer. "And don't you ever forget it."

Before their lips could touch again, Hazel once more started yipping.

"No play!" she said. "New dogs."

"New dogs?" Nancy glanced down at Hazel. "What new dogs?" Hazel started barking and writhing in Nancy's grasp. "Hazel, stop. Stay!"

"I stay," Hazel said, still barking furiously. "Down. I stay."

Nancy quickly lowered herself to the ground as Hazel managed to wriggle free from her grasp so that the dog wouldn't hurt herself as she launched herself from Nancy's arms.

"Stay off the platform," Nancy said. "Stay off the circle. Circle danger. Understand?"

"No circle," Hazel said, giving the platform a wide berth as she ran around. "No bye-byes."

"Bye-byes?" Tarn asked.

"It's what I say when we're going to take a ride in a car." Nancy pointed at the platform and said, "We were at the platform in Earth's solar system, then we went through that blue space, and now we're here."

"Blue space?"

"Oh yeah," Nancy shook her head as if she was rattling something loose, then smiled. "I should have put those together. We went through blue space."

"That's not possible. You have to have a ship to travel through blue space."

"Well… I haven't been through blue space on a ship yet, but from how Olivia and Lian described it to me, that's where we were."

"I only saw a void."

"Really?" Nancy's brow furrowed. "Does that mean you didn't see the dragons, either?'

"Dragons?"

"Or Der'Eghonians or whatever you call them. There were all these beautiful swirling blues, with red dragon silhouettes flying in the distance."

Tarn's mind was racing as he tried to sort things out. He could feel he was right at the edge of an epiphany that would make all the pieces fall into place. He just needed the last key.

"I thought I was hallucinating at first, but now I'm not so sure," Nancy said. "I mean, I guess I had just seen the dragon on this armband."

"That's it," he nearly shouted. He clasped her arm and lifted it closer so that he could see the armband more closely. "The armband is the key."

"What key?"

"The key to the platform. It's a transit platform."

"A what platform?"

"A transit platform. It's a theoretical device somewhat like a teleportation pad."

Nancy's eyes shifted to the side as she considered Tarn's words. "Why did it blow everybody else up, then?"

"Because they weren't wearing this." He lifted her arm a little higher. "It must be Der'Eghonian technology. There are obscure legends in our most ancient texts that say they can travel through blue space without ships. Maybe this is what those were referencing."

"Oh cool." Nancy's eyes widened as she stared at the armband. "I should give it back to you, then."

"Keep it on," Tarn said. "It's probably what protected us."

"So, Norem was trying to find a way to send people through blue space."

"If he only had one armband, I doubt Norem would ever trust anyone else to use it," Tarn said.

Nancy rolled her eyes, as if the thought of not trusting people was stupid. And yet...

"He probably gave it to Zakarri for safekeeping," Tarn said.

"Or Zakarri just stole it to have leverage."

Tarn tried to tamp down his surprise. She looked up at him and shrugged.

"I understand that certain individuals are not to be trusted," Nancy said. "But because of who they've shown themselves to be, not because of what they are. Tobek? I totally trust that guy. Norem? No way. They both started out as Tau Ceti."

"You really are going to try to become friends with whoever finds us here, aren't you?" Tarn scowled. He was more thinking out loud than expecting a response, but Nancy answered him anyway.

"See? You're understanding me better already." She smiled and batted her eyelashes at him, exuding such confidence that part of him believed she would be successful. Only part, though. He was still most focused on getting them out of this safely.

"Maybe we should just jump back on and return to Ceres," Tarn said. "That would be safest."

"Safest for me." Nancy shook her head. "Not for you. I can't take that chance."

"Then you go through and leave me here. They wouldn't dare risk angering the Cygnians by hurting me— even if they were capable of that."

"I would never leave you here."

Tarn smiled. Nancy scowled.

"What?" she said.

"It's nice to know you care."

"Of course, I care." Her scowl deepened. "You're my soulmate, like it or not."

"But you're liking it more," he said.

"You have your moments. When you aren't hating on people I care about just because they're Scorpiians or whatever."

"A Scorpiian assassin," he said.

"Retired." She was quiet for a moment, then shook her head.

"What?"

"It's just. Would it make a difference to you if he weren't an assassin? If he was just some random Scorpiian you knew nothing about?"

He tried to clamp down on his instinctive response, but from the way the skin around her eyes tightened and her lips pulled into a deeper frown, he hadn't been successful.

"Forget it," she said. "I shouldn't have asked a question I didn't want the answer to."

"Nancy, please. I'm trying."

"I know," she said. "Just… keep thinking of yourself as a crystal. Crystals seem set in their form, but they grow. They're open to receiving light, and that light changes them and changes everything around them. Think of how much more beautiful your existence can be if you open your heart—hearts—to all the possibilities around you."

Tarn's hearts were pounding a steady, strong beat. How could his soulmate be so pure? So perfect? Nancy had already opened his hearts. Soulmates balanced each other, completed each other. She *was* his light and he would do everything in his power to open himself to her influence.

"Oh my gosh, Hazel," Nancy said, suddenly looking past Tarn. "What is she doing?"

He turned to see the small dog digging at a blank section of wall. Tarn finally spotted the double door leading into the chamber, just as it was in the Ceres base. The door was nowhere near the little dog. He couldn't see any reason for her to be digging where she was, but her little claws scrabbled at the metal of the wall.

"New dogs," Hazel repeated.

"What does that mean?" Nancy asked.

Anxiety knotted Tarn's stomach again. The Centaurans weren't just shifters. They were wolf-shifters. Was Hazel somehow able to sense them? To his knowledge the Centaurus system only had one inhabitable planet, Centaurus-10. It was their homeworld.

"You are putting off some really troubling emotions right now," Nancy said.

"I wouldn't hide my concern from you if I could. You need to understand that we are in a great deal of danger. If a Centauran comes into this room and sees you, they might not give us a chance to explain that you aren't Sadirian. We might have to fight."

"No, we might have to increase the power to our shields or something," she said. "Besides, don't they also look just like Earthlings and Sadirians? Maybe we can make them think I'm a lost Centauran or something."

"They'll know."

"There is always a way to find a common ground," she insisted. "Always."

Once more, Tarn was struck by just how amazing his soulmate was. Her conviction and optimism more than anything else made her the most beautiful sentient he had ever encountered.

"Okay, those emotions are much nicer." She smiled as she slowly approached him, her own emotions clearly conveying her intentions. Tarn's spine plates began to rise for a much more pleasant reason.

Hazel ran between them, barking. "No play! New dogs."

Nancy let out a frustrated grunt. "What new dogs?"

"There." Hazel turned her head toward the wall.

"It's just a wall, Hazel." Nancy said. She walked closer to it, gesturing to the blank surface. "See? Just a wall."

Hazel lowered her head and sniffed the ground. Tarn could barely make out the word, "Here," whispered over her low growl.

A cloud of pale white light emerged from the wall, followed by another and another. Nancy backed away, her eyes wide. The clouds swirled above them in slow circles. They lowered, breaking formation to travel around the room, like glowing wisps of energy.

"Tarn..." Nancy backed farther from the wall. She went to reach for Hazel, but the little dog leapt out of her grasp.

"No up," Hazel said, barking and wagging her tail. "Play."

"Now is not the time, Hazel," Nancy said.

The little dog ignored her, lowering the front of her body and barking more loudly. "New dogs."

"Wait, these are the new dogs?" Nancy turned toward Tarn. "Is this some kind of life form on this planet?"

"I'm not sure. We've only ever encountered the Centaurans and know almost nothing about their homeworld."

"Play," Hazel said, barking as one of the wisps of energy circled almost in reach, then quickly moved away. "New friends."

"Well, Hazel likes them," Nancy said. "So, I like them, too." She stepped forward and said, "I come in peace." She laughed and glanced at Tarn over her shoulder. "I always wanted to say that."

The wisps drew closer. Tarn's unease grew.

"Nancy…"

"Don't worry. Sometimes, you have to be the first to trust. I'm not afraid to take that first step." She reached out toward one of the wisps. "I'd like to be your friend," she said, in a gentle voice. "I want so much to understand you."

The closest wisp narrowed where it was nearest to Nancy, reaching out with an armlike tendril that mirrored her gesture. Tarn held his breath, willing himself to trust. Of all the things that might comfort him, Zemanni's words rang through his mind. 'If she thinks she can handle something, she probably can.'

Tarn prayed to the Maker that he was right.

Chapter Nine

Nancy's heart was pounding in her chest. Her mouth had gone dry and a constant wave of energy shot up and down her spine. She knew that last was from Tarn. His fear was almost as strong as her excitement. *Almost.* She refused to let it cloud her judgment when meeting these new life forms.

Not even Tarn knew what these were. She was about to make literal first contact with a new species of alien. Hazel had the best judgment of character of anyone Nancy knew. She trusted her little companion. The cloud of silver light drew closer, nearly touching Nancy's outstretched fingers as the others circled them.

"Hi," Nancy said, laughing.

Through the translucent being, she saw the large double doors that led into the chamber slide open. A tall man strode through, broad-shouldered and packed with lean muscle that she could clearly see through gaps in his loose clothing. He was clean-shaven, showcasing the strong angles of his jaw and cheekbones. His eyes widened and his mouth dropped open as he saw her.

"Stop!" he shouted.

She started to pull back, but the cloud in front of her rushed forward, engulfing her before she could move. Nancy yelped in surprise as warmth—not cold—surrounded her. It was like she was getting a steam bath in every individual pore, her muscles relaxing as the warmth suffused first her skin, then deeper, all the way through to her bones. Somehow, the sensation didn't stop there.

She blinked as the chamber filled with crystal lattices. No, not crystal. Ice. The structures didn't move as she turned her head. It wasn't the chamber, it was her eyes themselves. What was happening to her?

A rush of cool energy flooded her, carrying strength unlike anything she'd ever felt. If she wanted, she was certain she could leap across the chamber without the help of her Cygnian wristbands. She could pick up this stranger and toss him in the air like a child. She laughed, staring down at her hands and wiggling her fingers. Her skin was glowing silver.

"Mom! Mooooooooooom!" Hazel was barking at her feet, wagging her tail like crazy. The silver light extended from Nancy to the little dog, encircling her in a protective glow that Nancy didn't understand, but didn't fear.

"*Hello.*" Nancy gasped as a feminine voice echoed through her mind. "*I want to understand you, too.*"

"*Who are you?*" Nancy thought. She wanted to ask, '*What* are you,' but would save that question for later.

Nancy sensed confusion, but then a wave of emotions flowed through her, along with memories. *Her* memories.

She saw herself walking through a snowstorm, looking down into her coat at Hazel when she was just a little puppy. It had been so cold. Nancy wanted to be sure to keep her warm and had tucked the little fur ball into her coat until they were safely back home. The same love and protectiveness she'd felt at the time rushed through her, as if she was there when it was happening. The memory changed to Nancy sitting around laughing with her friends, camaraderie and belonging coursing through her.

Tears blurred her vision, breaking up the lattice of ice as she felt her mother's arms around her when she was just a small child, holding her close and whispering in her ear how much she loved her and that she would always take care of her and protect her and help her to achieve her dreams and goals.

Nancy sniffed and let out a small laugh. Whatever was talking to her, the warmth and love the being was putting off was undeniable.

"*The answer to both of your questions—I am* zyln," the voice said, softly.

"What have you done to her?" Tarn shouted, in a much louder voice. He launched himself at the new man.

"Stop," Nancy yelled. Tarn either didn't hear or ignored her.

"*Typical,*" Nancy thought.

"*He is Cygnian,*" the voice responded in Nancy's mind as she—they—rushed forward to try to help.

"*So, I'm supposed to tolerate him attacking people?*"

"*He does not need to fight. He needs to* act. *We will help him understand. We will help both of them.*"

"Holy…" Nancy skidded to a stop as the stranger began to glow silver. The light pulsed over his skin, nearly blinding her. It grew and shifted, along with his form. In a final burst, it vanished, leaving behind an enormous white-coated wolf.

"What the h—" She broke off in a scream as Tarn kept up his momentum, grappling with the beast and twisting around, somehow flipping over him. Tarn lifted the wolf from the ground, carrying it with him. As soon as Tarn's feet hit the ground again, he threw the wolf across the room. The enormous beast hit the wall with a bone-jarring impact, then fell to the ground.

Tarn turned to her briefly. "Get back on the transit platform," he yelled. "I'll hold him off."

The wolf pushed himself up to stand, shaking his head. He pulled back his lips, revealing rows of glistening, sharp teeth. Ice spread out from beneath his paws, coating the floor and crawling up the wall nearest him.

"Oh, that is so cool," Nancy murmured.

"Nancy!" Tarn yelled, an odd tremor to his voice. "Grab Hazel and run."

"Not without you," she yelled back.

Frost tipped the ends of Tarn's hair. He shook his head with an odd, jerky movement. Shards of ice rose up from the ground, encasing his feet. His skin was paling. Nancy glanced down to see Hazel absolutely unbothered by the cold. Nancy was perfectly warm as well. Were Tarn's environmental shields failing? She quickly struck her wristbands together and hummed the note that connected hers to his, then switched to the tone to increase power to his shields.

They weren't even on.

"Oh my god," she said. "What are you doing?"

"P...pr... protecting you," he chattered. "S...saving p...p...power."

"Stop it. I'm fine." Nancy let out a disgusted grunt, then activated his environmental shielding herself.

Gold light swept over his skin, only visible for a moment. He let out a sigh, the frost on his hair and skin evaporating instantly. With one last glance, as if to reassure himself that she was, in fact, fine, he kicked his feet, shattering the ice surrounding them. He turned back to the wolf, crouching low.

The wolf wasted no time in attacking. He leapt through the air, his claws easily finding purchase on the ice coating the floor. Tarn leapt forward to meet him, but his boots slipped and he nearly lost his balance. The wolf hit Tarn's chest, taking him to the ground and biting at his face. Tarn grabbed the fur on the wolf's neck, holding him back. The beast's vicious jaws snapped inches from his face.

"Stop, please," Nancy yelled, her eyes glittering. "Please, we have to stop them."

"*We will,*" the voice in her mind said. "*Will you trust me?*"

"Yes," Nancy said. "Of course." She didn't know why it was true, but she felt it with every fiber of her being.

"*Then let go.*" Warmth suffused the *zyln's* voice.

Nancy closed her eyes as she took in a deep breath, then let it out slowly. The warmth from the *zyln* spread through Nancy's body, relaxing her muscles, her bones, and her joints. She felt as though she was stretching, even though she hadn't moved. As she exhaled again, she drifted forward, lifting her arms to catch herself as she fell onto all fours. She opened her eyes to see giant white paws beneath her. She scrabbled back, the paws slipping out from under her in her haste. *Her* paws?

"*Oh my god,*" she thought. "*This is me. I'm a wolf.*"

"*Yes,*" the *zyln* said. "*We have joined.*"

"*Joined?*"

"*We are one.*"

"*One?*" That sounded a lot like how she'd bonded with Tarn. But a soulmate bond felt different than this.

"*I will be with you always,*" the *zyln* thought.

"*Wait, is this like… permanent?*"

"*You will not have to remain in this form.*"

"*But you'll be with me… forever?*"

"*Yes. It is the way of* zyln. *I will protect you and give you strength and power. We have bonded.*"

Nancy reeled at the thought of having an alien consciousness living inside of her. First bonding with a Cygnian, and now being sort of... possessed by an alien... It was a bit overwhelming. At the same time, the idea of being a space werewolf was insanely cool. Either way, she didn't have time to freak out.

"*What do I do now?*" Nancy thought.

"*Now, we stop Garreth.*"

"*We. Right. Who's Garreth, though?*"

"*The other wolf. We must not harm him, but we must help him understand.*"

Nancy didn't understand everything herself, but that wasn't going to keep her from acting. She flexed her claws, digging into the ice coating the floor, then launched herself at the wolf attacking Tarn—at Garreth. She angled her head just as she hit him in the side with her shoulder. Both of them rolled across the room, sliding on the slick floor. Garreth wriggled to his back, getting his paws beneath Nancy. He shoved her away, sending her hurtling through the air. She hit the ground ready, claws carving deep gauges in the thickening ice.

Waves of mist rose around her. She somehow knew it was cold, but she didn't feel it. She quickly glanced over at Hazel, knowing small dogs were more susceptible to temperature extremes than larger ones. Hazel didn't seem bothered by the cold at all. She was trying to run toward Tarn, her paws slipping beneath her so that she was running in place. It would have been comical if Nancy wasn't in the fight of her life.

"I will protect your foster," the *zyln* said. *"The cold of this planet will harm neither you nor Hazel. Focus on your soulmate."*

Reassured that at least Hazel was out of harm's way for the moment, Nancy turned her attention back to the fight. Garreth was on his feet again, his eyes wide as he stared at Nancy. She lowered her head to the ground, a low growl vibrating in her throat. The fur along her spine was sticking up the way a Cygnian's spine plates would. Her muscles were filled with strength, with power. The Cygnian wristbands had adjusted size to remain on her wrists—forearms…whatever. She wasn't sure if they were still enhancing her strength and shielding her. Still, she was certain she could take Garreth down. Heck, she could probably give Tarn a run for his money in this form. But that wasn't her. *This* wasn't her. Was it?

"It is part of you," the *zyln* said. *"Part of everyone. But not the strongest part. You choose kindness and understanding."*

"I choose," Nancy repeated in her mind.

She stood straighter, slowly approaching Garreth. Tarn was on his feet again as well. He looked back and forth between Nancy and the other wolf, his features pinched with worry. She remembered what Lian and Olivia had told her about projecting emotions when words wouldn't do. Nancy focused on sending him reassuring energy, letting him feel her confidence and optimism. They were going to sort this out. All of them.

For all she knew, she was making first contact between Earth and the Centaurans. If they could come to a peaceful resolution here, maybe it would help Garreth realize that the Centaurans could make peace with the Coalition as well. She wasn't sure it would make a difference in the larger scheme of things, but she had to try.

Garreth let her draw closer than Nancy expected. Tarn was a tight ball of worry behind her. It was building into something stronger. Something darker. She narrowed her eyes at him and growled. Tarn's spine plates rose and he took a step forward, but then he blanched and paused. Did he even know it was her? Surely he had to feel their connection? At the same time, he seemed so uncertain.

She kept her head high and turned back to Garreth, holding his gaze even though she didn't know if it was a sign of trying to assert dominance among his people. She wanted him to know that she wasn't a pushover without offending him. For all she knew, he might be a high-ranking Centauran, but Nancy was not from his planet. Respect was one thing. Submissiveness was another. She lowered her head in a slight bow that she hoped conveyed that, keeping eye contact the entire time.

Garreth was still growling. She wasn't sure if he realized it. Nancy let out a little snort in an attempt to draw his attention to it. He blinked and shook his head slightly, then narrowed his eyes, his growl deepening.

"How do I make him understand that I don't want to fight?" Nancy thought, hoping her *zyln* could help.

"We would normally show submission," her *zyln* replied.

"Absolutely not." The vehemence of her thought even surprised Nancy. *"I'm offering him friendship, not submission."*

A ringing sound like wind chimes sounded in her mind. Was that laughter? Delight trickled through Nancy from her *zyln*.

"You have much to teach us," the *zyln* said.

"First, I need to get him to listen." Nancy sighed. *"Which I guess means I need to be able to talk. Can you change me back, please?"*

"Of course."

Warmth coursed through her again. Silver light filled her vision. Nancy felt herself crouching, then rising up onto her human legs. She wiggled her fingers as her paws turned back into her normal hands. Energy flooded her, every cell filled with life. It was exhilarating.

"Well, that was incredible." Nancy smiled and shook herself, laughing. "But now we need to stop fighting so we can sort this out. And for us to do that, you need to turn back to your other form. Unless you want the three of us to kick your butt."

Her excitement ebbed as Tarn's worry turned to rage laced with… lust? She glanced over her shoulder at him. He was staring at her body.

"Oh no." Nancy looked down to see that her clothes were gone. She turned to where she had been standing when she transformed and saw a pile of shredded fabric. "Not again. That's like twice in twenty-four hours!"

She hurried over to Tarn and stood behind him, working at the laces on his tunic. "A little help?"

He quickly removed the garment and handed it to her, never turning away from Garreth. The distrust and worry coming off of Tarn was like a miasma. As much as she wanted to tell him to cut it out, she understood where he was coming from a lot better in this situation. Garreth hadn't made a move, but he could still attack them at any time. Nancy pulled the tunic on and began tightening the laces to help it fit her better—or at least cover more. The garment engulfed her.

She peered around Tarn's side and said, "Would you please turn back, Garreth? You're making Tarn nervous. But we are done fighting." She made sure to address that last part to Tarn as much as to Garreth.

Nancy ducked back behind Tarn and finished the last touches on her makeshift attire. Smoothing her hands over it, she smiled as she inspected her work. When she stepped to Tarn's side, Garreth was standing across the room, making his own final adjustments on his clothes. They hadn't been damaged at all when he transformed.

"Okay, you have got to show me those designs," Nancy said.

"Who are you?" Garreth demanded in a harsh tone.

Nancy didn't let it bother her. She let loose her brightest smile and said, "I'm Nancy. This is Tarn. He's my soulmate."

A shiver flowed up her spine. Part of it was Tarn's pleasure at her claiming him so openly. She had to admit, most of it was her own.

"As you can see, he's obviously Cygnian," she said. "And my being his soulmate classifies me as a Cygnian as well. Anyway, I know I look Sadirian, which is probably freaking you out, but I also look just like you or... actually the Tau Ceti, now that I'm thinking about it. I wasn't genetically engineered to look this way. I'm from Earth. You might have heard of it." She cocked her head to the side and amped up her smile. "It's the planet where all the refugees are heading after you destroy their homes."

One of the muscles in Garreth's cheek started to twitch. More ice and cold mist flowed off from him. She'd gotten under his skin with that last part.

Good.

"*Garreth does not agree with his leader's course of action,*" her *zyln* said. "*Many of us do not.*"

"We have a saying on Earth," Nancy said, as much to her *zyln* as to Garreth. "'Actions speak louder than words.' I'm a fan of both, actually." She cast a quick glance at Tarn. "What we say is important. Our words are how we can express our thoughts. But without the conviction to act, it's all just…" She waved her hand, disrupting the mist closest to her. "Hot air."

"So, you've chosen an act of war," Garreth said.

"What? No." Nancy shook her head vehemently. "Our getting here was an accident. At least, it looks that way on the surface. But now that we're here, maybe we can make some good come of it. Maybe we can work at understanding each other better and finding a way forward in peace."

Chapter Ten

What was happening? Tarn should never have let Nancy make contact with that mist. He should stop her from trying to forge peace with this Centauran as well. Except... the mist had changed her. Transformed her. She had... shifted. Tarn needed to know what had happened to her. For that, he needed this Centauran to cooperate.

He would *make* the Centauran cooperate.

"Oh my god, we are done fighting," Nancy said, turning to glare at him. "Didn't I just say that? You need to stop it with all those fighty thoughts."

In the thick of battle, the obvious choice had seemed to be to have Nancy and Hazel go back through blue space to return to Ceres. Now that Tarn had calmed, he realized the danger that presented. Luck had guided them safely through the first time. Now that Nancy had... changed... would it also alter her ability to traverse that expanse safely? He couldn't risk it. They would find another way out of this.

"Nancy," Tarn said, his tone as full of warning as the caution radiating out from him through their bond. Nancy had to feel it. But all he sensed from her was that damned optimism and confidence that was both intoxicating and—at the moment—terrifying.

"Cygnians are not spies," Garreth said.

How had Nancy known his name?

Tarn puffed up his chest, his hands clenching at his sides. At least this Centauran knew that much. "We would never stoop to such a cowardly way of waging battle."

The shifter turned his attention to Nancy.

"You are Centauran," he said.

"What?" She scoffed. "No, I'm from Earth, a human. I just told you that a minute ago."

"Mom! Mom!" Hazel ran out from behind a makeshift console that had been set up against one of the walls.

Nancy knelt down and clapped her hands gently. "Hazel. Come here, baby."

Hazel's entire body was wriggling with excitement. "New dogs! New dogs!"

"I know, baby." Nancy picked Hazel up and held her close to her chest while the little dog licked her chin. "I need you to settle down, though."

They looked back to Garreth to see his eyes wide.

"That... is your child?" he said.

Nancy laughed, though the sound was tighter than usual. She adjusted her hold on Hazel to keep the dog safe but also control her wriggling.

"She's my little fur baby," Nancy said.

"Are all Earthlings like that when they're born?" Garreth said.

Nancy's eyes widened and then she burst out laughing. "What? No."

Tarn stepped in quickly, trying to avoid another confrontation. "Hazel isn't... Okay, she actually is an Earthling, but Nancy is human and Hazel is a dog. Dogs are a companion animal that become part of human families."

Nancy's ire hit him before she spoke. "Exactly."

"Humans have limited experience of other worlds," Tarn said, pointedly. "They don't know how many species begin life as a seemingly completely different form and undergo transformations throughout their lifespan that are unrecognizable from one stage to the next."

"Oh." She grimaced, but he could sense she was somewhat placated. "That's true. But humans also don't like it when other people speak for them." She smiled and batted her eyelashes at him in an expression that was somehow both enticing and unsettling. How could she challenge him just with her eyelashes? "At least, this human does," she said.

"Do humans also have their own *zyln*?" Garreth said

Tarn's brow furrowed. "What's a *zyln*?"

"Oh, I'm sorry," Nancy said. "You don't know something about an alien race? Wow, it would feel so awful if someone pointed that out and rubbed your face in it."

Tarn's spine plates had just begun to settle, but now they rose again. She was challenging him relentlessly. It was infuriating and... arousing. From the way her cheeks flushed, he had to guess that she was feeling the same.

"But to answer your question," Nancy said, "No, we don't have *zyln* on Earth or any life forms remotely like them."

Garreth shook his head. "Only Centaurans can bond with *zyln*."

"What is a *zyln*?" Tarn repeated, his voice sharp with impatience.

Nancy waved at him dismissively while she answered his question instead of Garreth. "They're energy beings who coinhabit this planet along with the Centaurans. They keep the Centaurans and their children safe from the cold until the children are old enough to join with their own *zyln*. Once they do, they can shift into wolf forms and—" Nancy suddenly looked aside, speaking as if she was talking to someone Tarn couldn't see. "Oh my god, I have ice powers? You're kidding. That is so cool!"

"Nancy," Tarn shouted. She started, her attention snapping back to his. His hearts clenched as he spoke, asking a question that he was sure he didn't want answered. "Is one of those things inside of you?"

"'One of those *things*?'" Her gaze intensified and Tarn knew he had offended her before her disappointment could reach him through their bond. "*Zyln* are sentient life forms, not *things*."

Wariness and something else flowed out through their bond. She felt a vulnerability he had never sensed from her before. One that made him want to wrap his arms around her and promise to keep her safe. But the wariness she felt was directed at *him*. His breath caught in his chest at the concept. How could she fear what he thought of her?

"And yes," she said, her voice smaller than he'd ever heard it before. "One of them has joined with me."

"'Joined,'" he said. "But it isn't permanent, right?"

Her frown deepened. She didn't answer.

"Right?" he repeated. The sinking feeling in his stomach intensified, as did Nancy's dread.

"Once a *zyln* has joined with another sentient, their presence is permanent," Garreth said. "However, they can only bond with Centaurans."

"And apparently Earthlings." Nancy said, a smile painted on her face that Tarn could tell she didn't feel.

Not entirely, anyway. But he could sense her building back her optimism one thought at a time, pulling herself up from the worry that had enshrouded her.

"How did you get here?" Garreth demanded.

"Through the transit platform," Nancy said.

"Nancy!" Tarn's warning was too late. He wasn't ready to share that information with Garreth. The Centaurans were probably working with the Tau Ceti to develop this technology. But from the look of surprise on Garreth's face, Tarn wondered if he actually didn't know what the platform was.

"A transit platform?" Garreth repeated. "To your homeworld?"

"Technically, it's to another astronomical body in our solar system," Nancy said. "But yes, it does connect to our home system."

"Nancy, it is unwise to share this information with—" Tarn stopped as Nancy glared at him.

"Garreth is not our enemy," Nancy said. She turned back to him with that forced smile. "He is our new friend. Just like... like my *zyln* is our new friend."

She glanced uneasily at Tarn, but quickly turned her attention back to Garreth. Her worry wasn't about Garreth or even the energy being who was inhabiting her body. Her worry was directed toward Tarn. It was as if she didn't know where she stood with him. As if she was suddenly unsure of their bond. Tarn was desperate to ask her what was wrong, to soothe her worries. But not while there was a potential threat in the room with them—on a planet full of threats.

"Wherever you are from, being accepted by a *zyln* makes you a Centauran," Garreth said. "But that doesn't make us friends."

"Give it time," Nancy said, her smile warming a bit. "It can take a while to get used to me, but I bet we'll be besties before you know it."

"We truly didn't mean to trespass on your homeworld," Tarn said. "And we will leave the moment we can secure transport back."

"The transit platform only works one way?" Garreth asked.

Tarn hesitated to respond. He didn't know whether that was accurate or not. Sending Nancy back through could have been even more dangerous than he'd realized. His hearts sped at the thought of the risk he had almost exposed her to. The idea of his soulmate hurtling through blue space alone without even a ship to protect her... His spine plates rose, their shimmering vibration sending ripples through the misty air surrounding him.

"Tarn, remember what I said earlier." Nancy cast a hesitant, yet encouraging smile at him. "Sometimes, we have to be the ones to trust first."

Tarn shook his head. "We don't know. Until we went through it just now, we had no idea what would happen."

After a brief pause, Garreth said, "You're very brave to put yourselves at risk like that in the name of discovery."

"It was actually kind of an accident." Nancy laughed. "Hazel ran toward the platform on the other end and we ran after her. I couldn't quite grab her in time to keep us all from landing on it. On Earth, we'd say this was a case of having more luck than sense. But now that we know what it does, we can just hop back on and head home."

"If it even *will* take you home," Garreth mused.

A delicate furrow appeared between Nancy's brows. "What?"

"We had determined that this platform is a gateway directly into blue space." Garreth's eyes became unfocused as if he was thinking through several things at once. "If it's actually a transit platform, there might be more than two of them linked throughout the galaxy. Or even the universe. Yours sent you here, but ours might send you to a completely different location."

"Oh." Nancy looked dejected. "I hadn't thought of that."

"He's right," Tarn said. "And the more I think about it, it's too dangerous for us to try a return trip anyway. Just because we traveled here safely doesn't mean we could do so again."

"I guess we don't want to end up like those poor test subjects." Nancy shuddered.

Garreth instantly stiffened. "Test subjects? What test subjects?"

"The Tau Ceti," she said. "They used their own people to test the transit platform at the base on Ceres."

A cloud of mist billowed out from Garreth's skin. Glowing silver light pulsed over him. His features contorted with the most vicious hatred and rage Tarn had ever seen. Tarn couldn't tell if the Centauran was about to shift or not. He stepped in front of Nancy, regardless, urging her back toward the closest wall.

"Tarn, what have I told you about trying to protect me?" she said, deftly ducking under his arm. "Garreth, please calm down. Just breathe through it."

Nancy took an exaggerated breath in, then blew it out in the same manner. She waved her hand in a circle, as if encouraging Garreth to do the same. Remarkably, the Centauran began mimicking her, breathing along with her. The mist subsided a bit, but the rage on his features was still evident.

"Tell me about the test subjects," Garreth said.

"You don't know?" Tarn asked.

"Of course I don't know." Garreth snarled as he spoke. "That's why I'm asking."

"We're sorry." Nancy's voice was painfully gentle. "We thought you did, since you're working with the Tau Ceti and they were experimenting with another transit platform just like this one back in Earth's solar system."

"Your 'allies' didn't bother to tell you?" Tarn enquired.

"They knew about our gateway—our transit platform," Garreth said. "The *zyln* have been using it as a portal to blue space and exploring, then coming back and communicating what they discover with us, but we considered it much too dangerous to try to send a corporeal life form through. We didn't know there was another platform in the Sol system."

Nancy was uncharacteristically quiet. Tarn stepped in

to spare her from having to explain the horrors they had found there.

"You were wise to be cautious," Tarn said. "When we destroyed the Tau Ceti base on Ceres, we took possession of their transit room. There was evidence of experiments done on multiple life forms. Experiments that ended in their gruesome deaths."

A tendon started to twitch in Garreth's jaw again. "Present your evidence."

Tarn glanced over at Nancy. She gave him a quick encouraging nod. He lifted his arms and slowly struck his wristbands together, then hummed the notes necessary to bring up their holoprojection function. With the thickness of the frosty air, the images appeared grainy. Nancy lifted her hand and took in a deep breath, then slowly let it out. As she did, the air surrounding Tarn cleared.

Maker, whatever had happened to her had truly given her the powers of a Centauran. Tarn didn't know how it worked, but they could manipulate the temperature, generating extreme cold. They could freeze opponents instantly, encasing them in ice. And that was in addition to their ability to change forms.

They were shifters. *Nancy* was a shifter.

His hearts sank at the thought, but he shook off the dark sensation. She was still Nancy. His soulmate. He had already opened his mind to change. This only sped up the process of his growth. Of *shifting* his own paradigms.

Tarn had been raised in the temples of Cygnus-Prime. His mother was Alpha Priestess of all Cygnians. Her teachings glorified the crystalline structures that made up their world and disparaged anything that didn't 'hold true to one form.' But Nancy was right. Crystals did grow. And his people *were* changing.

The Maker herself had altered Tarn so that he might be able to have children with an Earthling—with Nancy. If Queen Ehmach and King Korvin hadn't been open to change, if they had not been open to modifying their DNA to be more compatible with other species, the Cygnians would have become extinct within a few more generations. Just as their bodies were becoming more malleable, their beliefs needed to evolve as well.

Tarn was sick of the Cygnians remaining neutral in the conflicts the rest of the galaxy faced. They stood by while the High Council abused their power and controlled the citizens of the Coalition of Planets in horrifying ways. They didn't step in when the Tau Ceti invaded other homeworlds, using the sentients who had lived there as a *food source*. Now, they stood by while the Tau Centauran Assembly destroyed every safe harbor for the people of the Coalition.

The Assembly had already killed everyone on the High Council, throwing the Coalition into disarray. They had destroyed Sadr-4, the Sadirian homeworld, and every single colony, space station, and dome-world the Sadirians had established. Their home system was a dead husk. Still, it wasn't enough. They had been working their way through the galaxy, destroying every Sadirian outpost they could find. The only genuine safe harbors left to the Sadirians were in the Sol system.

The Sol system... Where the other transit platform is located.

A horrible concept rose in Tarn's mind. One as terrifying as it was brilliant.

"I know what you're trying to do," Tarn said, dread pooling in his stomach. He glared up at Garreth. "I know your plan, and we will stop you."

Chapter Eleven

Whatever Tarn knew—or thought he knew—it was enraging him more than anything Nancy had ever felt from him. Instead of the amorphous anger and fear she'd felt from him before, this was glacial and much, much deadlier. She realized that Tarn had been holding back earlier, both with Garreth and Zemanni. But she had no doubt in that moment that if Garreth attacked again, Tarn would end him.

"*We must help them remain calm,*" her *zyln* said. "*Only then can they understand each other.*"

"*Tarn thinks he understands Garreth already,*" Nancy thought. "*That could be a problem.*"

"Our plan is to punish the Coalition for what they have done to our people," Garreth said. "Subjecting our soulmates to reckless experiments. Killing them. We will liberate the galaxy from their oppressive rule."

"I guess you didn't get the memo, but the galaxy has already been 'liberated,'" Nancy said. "You took care of that when you wiped out their home system and destroyed the High Council by blowing up their homeworld."

"The Coalition of Planets still exists," Garreth said.

"They still hold sway over much of the galaxy."

"They still exist because they're trying to take care of the people who remain." Nancy rolled her eyes, unable to hide her exasperation. "You executed their leaders—who might have had it coming—but the people left behind still need some kind of government to make sure their colonies get the food and resources they need and are protected."

"Don't waste your breath with this one," Tarn said, his voice low and even. "None of this will matter if they get their way. Every Sadirian in the galaxy will be dead."

"What?" Garreth and Nancy said at once.

Could the Centaurans hate Sadirians that much? Did they really want to kill them all? Tarn believed every word he said with a cold certainty. Nancy had to admit, his confidence was rattling her.

"*I do not believe the Centaurans wish to rid the galaxy of Sadirians,*" her *zyln* thought. "*Only of the influence of the High Council.*"

"*What if they think the only way to truly do that is to remove all of the Sadirians who followed the Council?*" Nancy thought. "*With the mind control the High Council performed on people without their knowledge, we're still finding sleeper agents ourselves.*"

Garreth was the first to recover. "We don't want to destroy all Sadirians. We're trying to free them from the tyranny of the Coalition."

"The Sadirians *are* the Coalition," Nancy said. "At

least, most of them, from what I know. I'm sorry they did experiments on Centaurans, but—"

"It wasn't Centaurans they killed, it was our soulmates." Garreth shook his head, his skin paling. "Some of our people bonded with Sadirians."

Nancy made a surprised little eeping sound. She had not expected that. But then, Earthlings could bond with Cygnians and were bonding with all sorts of aliens. Sadirians were similar to Earthlings, so why couldn't they also bond with other sentients?

"Can Sadirians bond with zyln?" Nancy thought.

"No, but we can extend our protective powers to bonded mates," her *zyln* thought. *"They could withstand incredible cold and even survive in the vacuum of space. I know of these experiments. The High Council was trying to find a way to replicate these abilities in Sadirians who weren't bonded with Centaurans. It... did not end well for the Sadirians or their Centauran soulmates, who were driven insane by the loss."*

The anger emanating from Tarn intensified. "That only makes what you have planned worse. If you have soulmates among the Sadirians, you've undoubtedly killed countless of their number during your war. How could you risk even a single one?"

Garreth paused, his teeth clenched tight. He shook his head brusquely. "We give our targets time to flee before destroying their infrastructures. The Coalition of Planets must not get a chance to regain their balance or they'll destroy us."

"My *zyln* told me what happened to your soulmates," Nancy said. "And it's terrible. Truly terrible. But that doesn't justify what you're doing. You've already won. You've destroyed the people behind the experiments. The people who were oppressing their population. The Coalition has changed since the High Council was destroyed. You're inflicting all this suffering for nothing."

"Not for nothing," Garreth said. "We're protecting our future."

"You're destroying their homes," Nancy said. "And people are dying."

"We knew there were risks." Garreth's voice was low and tight. "We're doing everything we can to ensure as many people escape as possible."

"So that they can be slaughtered in the Sol system," Tarn said.

"Wait, what?" This time, Nancy was the only one to speak. Garreth looked stunned, his eyes wide and his jaw going slack.

"They're herding all of the Sadirians into the Sol system," Tarn said. "Once there, the Assembly planned to teleport their soldiers into the asteroid belt through the transit platform on Ceres. They could bring in all the parts they needed to assemble weapons and ships plus people to assemble them and pilot them. My guess is they've been working on a reliable way to activate the transit platforms between these two systems."

Tarn turned back to Garreth, his voice dripping with contempt. "We're lucky we caught them before they succeeded. They could have brought millions of soldiers into the Sol system without anyone knowing. The asteroid field would have provided the perfect cover. Then, when they were ready, they could do a pincer maneuver, bringing in their forces from the edges of the solar system and attacking from within at the same time. Facing that many opponents, not even the Vegans would be able to keep everyone safe. They would fall back to Earth and focus on protecting their new homeworld, leaving the colonies established by Sadirians in other locations within the Sol system defenseless."

"Oh my god." Nancy could picture it in her mind. The plan was brilliant—and merciless. She turned back to Garreth, her own outrage joining with Tarn's. "Was that your plan? Is that who you are?"

"No," Garreth said. "No, we would never do that."

"Just like you'd never attack innocent civilian colonies?" Tarn said, stalking closer to Garreth. The Centauran was so stunned, he didn't even seem to notice. "Or leave the survivors to be dealt with by the Tau Ceti."

Nancy's stomach dropped at the thought. Her experience with the Tau Ceti was fairly limited. She knew Tobek and the other Tau Cygnian cyborgs, mostly through stories from Olivia and Lian. And she knew what had been done to them and other Tau Ceti soldiers stationed on the base. Most of the soldiers were probably just doing their jobs, but some, like Norem, were committing atrocities. If that was how they treated each other, how would they treat people they saw as their enemies?

"The Tau Ceti have more experience integrating conquered—" Garreth began.

"The Tau Ceti don't integrate," Tarn bellowed. "They devour. Do you know nothing of the people you have sided with?"

"We know that they were treated with more cruelty by the Coalition than anyone else," Garreth shouted back. "They were forced to modify their appearance, undergoing horrific and painful transformations to resemble their oppressors just to fit in and be treated with a semblance of dignity."

"They did experience more restrictions than other sentients brought into the Coalition." Tarn paused for a moment, then bellowed, "Because they're *cannibals*."

All the color fled from Garreth's face. "No, they... They're our allies. You're lying to try to tear us apart."

"I am a Cygnian," Tarn said, stalking even closer, till he towered over the other man, tall as he was. "We have no stake in this conflict, aside from the fact that your victims are gathering in numbers near the homeworld of our soulmates. Cygnians do not lie. And *we*, unlike you

Centaurans, protect our soulmates, no matter what. We don't leave them to be devoured by the people we have chosen as allies."

"*You believe him.*" Her *zyln's* thoughts were a weak echo in Nancy's mind. "*You believe what he is saying.*"

"*I do,*" Nancy thought. "*I wish I didn't. But I do. I know not all Tau Ceti are bad, but the ones who are...*" She shook her head.

"The Tau Ceti came to my planet." Nancy's voice sounded tinny to her own ears, as if she was hearing herself speak from far away. She was barely even aware she was talking, but words were coming out of her mouth. "They tried to establish spawning pools on Earth, but one of our scientists discovered them and stopped the Tau Ceti —with the help of Sadirians, before the High Council was even destroyed. They didn't have to help us, but they did."

"Spawning pools aren't—" This time, Nancy cut Garreth off.

"Some of the Tau Ceti were feeding off of humans," she said. "They didn't kill us outright, but they were literally feeding off of the chemicals that help us to be happy. Like vampires. Siphoning our blood and getting some kind of high from it. Not all of them." She looked at Tarn as she said the last part. "But enough. I believe what Tarn is saying."

Garreth's lip curled up in revulsion. Nancy couldn't blame him.

"We are not your enemies," she said, gently. "It might be hard to believe, but neither are the Sadirians."

"The Tau Ceti are our allies," Garreth said. "They know what our people have endured. They have shared what they endured—"

"Because they knew it would make you feel sympathy for them," Nancy said. "They probably have been through stuff, but nothing would justify what Norem was doing back on his base."

"Norem?" Garreth's brow furrowed and he angled his head to the side.

"Yes," Nancy said. "He was in charge of the base on Ceres."

Garreth looked at the transit platform intensely, as if he expected it to answer some question that Nancy couldn't fathom.

"For how long?" Garreth asked.

"I don't know." She looked to Tarn for help, but he just shrugged. "Months? Years?"

Garreth shook his head. "How long ago did you take over their base?"

"A few weeks I guess?" she said.

"Has anyone used the transit platform before you?"

"Only the people smeared on the walls," Nancy said. When Garreth flinched, she added, "Sorry."

"We think our transit platform was missing a key component," Tarn said. "An activator that we only recently acquired that links these two transit platforms."

"But that Norem had and could have used?" Garreth asked.

"Not for a while." Nancy tried to ignore the band of metal still wrapped around her upper arm, to avoid calling attention to it. She hugged Hazel closer.

"One of his colleagues took it from him," Tarn said. "A Scorpiian named Zakarri. He was seeking leverage to try to get one of Norem's test subjects back."

"Norem and Zakarri were working on the same project, but they had different goals," Nancy said. "Norem had his invasion plan, but Zakarri is just trying to get back his girlfriend, from what I've heard."

"That's oversimplifying things," Tarn said.

"Maybe you're overcomplicating them." She lifted her eyebrows and stared at him, daring him to contradict her.

"And Norem himself had no means of using the transit platform," Garreth said.

"No, Zakarri had the access component," Tarn said. "Probably for months. Unfortunately, we believe Norem was still able to escape before we attacked the base."

"Months," Garreth murmured. "He couldn't have used the transit platform for months, yet was on Ceres only weeks ago. This is all too unlikely." Garreth shook his head. He suddenly called out, "*Zyln*. Summon my research partner."

The wispy energy beings had been circling high above

their heads, blending in with the cold mists so well that Nancy hadn't even noticed them until they flew down and then through the wall.

"Describe this Tau Ceti to me," Garreth said. "This Norem."

"I never saw him." Nancy looked to Tarn again.

Tarn lifted his wrists and struck them together, activating their holoprojector function again. Rays of light flowed out, filling in the form of a man. He had short brown hair and a gaunt face with large, somewhat bulging eyes and a wide, thin mouth. Nancy remembered Lian saying that the Tau Ceti had evolved from something similar to a frog, but had genetically engineered themselves to look more like Sadirians to fit in better. Norem might be something of a throwback, compared to Tobek and the other Tau Ceti she had met. Then again, they'd been infused with Cygnian DNA, and that might have affected their appearance.

Garreth stared at the holoimage for a moment, the furrow of his brow deepening. "This is the Tau Ceti you say has committed atrocities at the Ceres base?"

"It is," Tarn said.

"What is it?" Nancy could tell Garreth was working through something—something important. He seemed more open to believing them, but there was a key piece of information they were missing. She was sure of it.

"Cygnians do not lie," Garreth said. "And yet, you

have laid blame on the one Tau Ceti who I know must be innocent."

Nancy arched her eyebrows. "Why is that?"

Before Garreth could answer, several *zyln* whisked back into the room followed by a man with short brown hair, a gaunt face, and a thin-lipped smile. He was dressed in a bronze encounter suit with copper trim and had a small bronze circlet resting on his forehead that seemed to be putting out some sort of bubble of energy around his head. Nancy looked at him, then back to the hologram, then back to him again.

"Garreth, your *zyln* friends are rather insistent I join you." Oddly, the man's words were laced with a southern accent. He froze when he saw them all, his eyes widening.

"This is my research partner," Garreth said. "We've worked together on our transit platform all day, every day for the past two years—including the past weeks and months."

"Oh crap," Nancy said.

"Norem," Tarn growled.

Chapter Twelve

How was this possible? Tarn's first thought was that Norem had been using the transit platform to travel back and forth, but Garreth had made a point of proving that Norem couldn't have done so for the last several months. If Norem had been here every day while Zakarri had the activator, how could he have also been at the Ceres base, commanding the Tau Ceti outpost there and performing his experiments?

"You didn't tell me we were expecting company," Norem said, recovering his composure somewhat. "And such surprising specimens, at that."

Tarn didn't miss the covetous look Norem cast at him. After they had obtained the lock box with the armband that controlled the transit portal, Zakarri had sought a new bargaining chip to use with Norem. The Scorpiian had abducted Bron, knowing Norem would love nothing more than a Cygnian specimen for his experiments. The Scorpiian hadn't cared if Bron was delivered dead or alive, knowing that Norem would be interested in having a Cygnian to use for his research either way. Bron would have died if a series of extremely unlikely circumstances hadn't aligned to save him. Looking at Norem's expression now, Tarn was certain the Tau Ceti scientist would still love to get his hands on a Cygnian.

Nancy stammered a bit, then smiled and said, "Okay, well this is really... strange."

Tarn could sense a mix of fear and determination coming from her. He stepped closer, but she caught his eye and shook her head. Then she turned back to Norem and beamed at him as she approached with her hand outstretched.

"I'm Nancy, and since you're interested in *specimens*, you should know I'm an Earthling," she said. "And since you're also *obviously* not the mastermind behind the Ceres base, it's good to meet you."

Norem arched an eyebrow, staring at her with obvious mistrust, before he reached out and grasped her hand, shaking it in the Earth-style greeting. Tarn's hearts beat quickly. He wasn't sure if it was his own fear or hers.

"Hmm," Nancy said. "Not a hologram."

Was that why she'd approached him? Tarn supposed it was good information to have, though he didn't like her being so close to the Tau Ceti. She could always activate her shielding if needed. It seemed to have deactivated itself when she transformed. Was there something about the energy of her *zyln* that interfered with her Cygnian wristbands? Dread crept out from Tarn's stomach at the thought, chilling him worse than the icy air. He knew nothing about the energy life form that had taken residence in his soulmate's body. What if it rendered her wristbands inoperable now that they were fully joined? How could Tarn protect her?

"An Earthling?" Norem said. "Now how in the world did you manage to get here?"

His eyes lingered on the armband she was wearing and he frowned briefly. Nancy followed his line of sight and intensified her smile.

"I'm guessing you already know," she said. "We picked this up from your friend, Zakarri. Oh, I'm sorry. With other-Norem's friend, Zakarri. But you wouldn't know anything about that, would you?"

Other-Norem...

An idea began to form in Tarn's mind. How the Tau Ceti could be in two places at once. Before he could fully grasp it, Hazel let out a low growl, distracting Tarn and drawing Norem's attention. His eyes widened yet again.

"A dog?" he said, finally noticing Hazel, who'd been tucked against Nancy's chest behind her arm. "You brought a dog here?"

"It wasn't exactly planned." Nancy shrugged.

"And she survived the trip through blue space," he mused. "All of you did."

He smiled brightly and shook his head, then reached up with his free hand and tapped the bronze metal encircling his forehead. He kept his grip on Nancy's hand, increasing

Tarn's unease. Part of the energy field the band was generating turned opaque, the tell-tale sign of a data screen being projected where only Norem could see.

"Nancy," Tarn warned. Something about the way Norem's smile deepened didn't sit well with Tarn. "Step away from him."

"I would love to," Nancy batted her eyes and cocked her head to the side. "But first he needs to give me back my hand. Unless he wants my Cygnian soulmate to rip his arm off for holding on for too long."

"Forgive my manners," Norem said. "It's just been such a long time since I've had the company of a beautiful Earthling. And one with such... delightful endorphins at that." His eyes rolled shut as he took in a long breath. "I can detect them even through my encounter suit. You truly are a joyful being."

A wave of unease rolled out from Nancy, crashing through Tarn, but she let out a breath instead of pulling away. Tarn started forward. The warning emotions she projected stopped him in his tracks. The room was growing colder. It wasn't coming from Nancy, but from Garreth. He was watching everything. Studying Norem, the situation. Suddenly, Tarn understood. Nancy was trying to get Norem to reveal himself. In fact, she might have already succeeded.

She stepped closer to Norem. The Tau Ceti's eyes softened, his lips curling away from his teeth.

"Delightful?" Nancy said, leaning even closer. "Or delicious?"

Norem smiled, revealing his sharpening canines. "Clever, Earthling. Not clever enough."

The next moment, Nancy was careening toward Tarn, doing her best to keep her grip on Hazel. The dog yelped as Norem shoved Nancy away. Tarn caught them both against his chest, turning to shield them as Norem drew a small blaster from somewhere in his suit. A ray of gold light shot out from it—not at Nancy or Tarn, but at Garreth. The Centauran lurched out of the way, but his foot caught on the edge of the transit platform. He fell toward the raised circular surface. Light engulfed him. Before he hit the platform, he vanished.

"No!" Nancy yelled. Tarn tightened his hold on her, keeping her close.

"Nancy," he shouted back. "Nancy! It's too late. He's gone."

Tears filled her eyes and she shook her head. She craned her neck around Tarn so that she could see Norem.

"He was your friend," she said. "How could you do that to him?"

Norem laughed. "He was a convenient tool—an opportunity. But now, a better one has come along."

Tarn straightened, pushing Nancy behind him. He was going to leap on Norem and tear him limb from limb.

"Whatever undoubtedly violent vision you have

brewing in that blue head of yours, I'd think better of it," Norem said.

Tarn stepped forward anyway. Norem only smiled. He slid the ray gun back into a pocket in his encounter suit, then lifted his arms. He held his left hand hovering over a blinking yellow button on the clunky bracer encasing his right forearm.

"You're fast, I'm sure," Norem said. "But not fast enough to keep me from detonating the explosives that I've hidden around the chamber."

"You wouldn't," Tarn said. "That would kill you."

"It would." Norem nodded. "You'd be fine, but your soulmate…" Norem hissed in a breath through his teeth. "She's an extraordinary specimen, but I doubt she would survive. Earthlings are rather delicate. And her little dog wouldn't stand a chance."

"That's where you're wrong," Nancy said.

Tarn's hearts picked up their beat. Norem hadn't figured out that Nancy was also Centauran now. She had been so open with Garreth, but surely she wouldn't give away that tactical knowledge.

"I have Cygnian wristbands with shielding that I'm sure can handle your little explosions," she said.

Tarn's relief that she had kept her secret was quickly washed away as she somewhat awkwardly struck her wristbands together while holding Hazel, then hummed the note to activate her shielding. The note that *should* have activated them. Her brow furrowed and she hummed the note again. Tarn watched for the flickering light that would let them know the shields were in effect. Nothing happened. She turned and glanced at Tarn and he shook his head, his hearts racing. How could he keep her safe without the wristbands? Hazel's collar should give her some protection, but depending on the blast, Tarn doubted its effectiveness.

"But you would die, too," Nancy restated.

"He doesn't care," Tarn said.

She turned to him, exasperated. "How could he not care?"

The pieces finally clicked in Tarn's mind. How Norem could be in two places at once without using the transit platform. One version here, studying its function. Another at the Ceres base, focusing on genetic experiments—on creating 'specimens' as he called them, that fit his needs perfectly.

"Because he's a clone," Tarn said.

Norem's eyebrows rose. "Well, now. And here I thought Cygnians were only good for fighting. Looks like at least one of you has a working brain. I can't wait to examine it."

"You'll never get a chance," Nancy said. "And besides... You know... Invulnerable. How could you even get to it?" She shuddered and shook her head.

"We have ways of getting inside your head that you've

never dreamed of," Norem said. "Sadirians did an excellent job focusing their technological development on controlling people's thoughts by downloading, uploading, and altering their memories. Add that in with our own advancements, and we are quite capable of bypassing any physiological barriers that might stand in our way. Even annoying little things like death." Norem reached up and tapped the circlet around his forehead. "There. Now I've uploaded my latest memory files to the primary repository. I truly have nothing at all to lose should you decide to be uncooperative."

"No one is being uncooperative." Nancy lifted her hand in a placating gesture. "We're talking and sort of... looking past the whole shooting Garreth onto the death platform."

Norem shrugged. "Who knows how it will affect a Centauran. Garreth never had the guts to send anyone through it, though their *zyln* could come and go as they pleased. Pesky things would have ratted me out in an instant if I'd brought in my own test subjects."

A glimmer of hope sprang up in Nancy. Tarn couldn't believe how much she already cared for Garreth. At the same time, his hearts warmed even more toward her. He had never met such a caring person.

"Well, see?" Nancy said. "You didn't even kill him. Maybe."

Norem laughed, keeping his hand poised above the

detonator. "You really are quite charming." He licked his lips, his expression softening in a way that made Tarn's spine plates stiffen. "It's been a long time since I've siphoned a human."

"Ew," she said. "Then again, if some human endorphins might make you a bit more... agreeable..."

What was she suggesting? Surely, she wouldn't let Norem feed off of her. Tarn wouldn't be able to stand by and let that happen. There was no way he could control himself if Norem so much as touched her again. Tarn's spine plates rose, their vibration resonating in the metal behind him.

Nancy turned to him and made an odd gesture where she lowered her hand. She projected calm at him. She must have a plan. He needed to trust her. She looked at Hazel and let out a low hum. Tarn was confused at first, but then he realized she was activating the shielding in Hazel's collar.

She handed the little dog to him and said, "Keep her safe for me."

"Nancy..." Tarn said.

Whatever she had planned it was terrifying them both. But her fear was mixed with determination. Her exhilaration with dread.

She turned back to Norem and smiled. "If you could excuse me for one moment while I make myself more presentable."

Norem's eyebrows rose. He glanced at Tarn, who was keeping himself frozen in place with every ounce of his strength. Hazel let out a little whine. Norem turned back to Nancy and licked his lips. A wave of disgust rolled out from her, but Tarn only knew because of their link. Her features still held that dazzling smile. Nancy walked to a large piece of equipment that stood out a bit from the wall. She lifted her arms and spun in a circle, as if showing Norem that she wasn't hiding anything, then ducked behind it, out of sight.

"What is she doing?" Norem asked. He seemed to be more talking to himself than expecting an answer. His eyes darted back to Tarn, skepticism plain on his expression.

Tarn knew. He felt it as a wave of cold shuddered down his spine. She was transforming. Shifting. And instead of being appalled, he was exhilarated. A ferocity unlike anything he'd sensed from her emanated from his soulmate. She was going to take Norem down. This moment of surprise might be their only chance.

"You can't think I would let you feed off of my soulmate," Tarn said, leaning against the nearest piece of equipment and feigning a nonchalance he didn't feel.

As Tarn had hoped, Norem mirrored his posture somewhat, lowering his hand a bit. "Honestly, I'm not sure what to make of either of you. I know this has to be some sort of diversion or plot, but I can't think of what you hope to gain by—"

Before he could finish his sentence, Nancy leapt over the mechanism she'd been hiding behind. Norem's eyes widened, his arms lowering for a moment in his shock. He brought them up to shield himself as she crashed into him, her paws hitting his shoulders and taking him to the ground. She snapped viciously at his face, never quite connecting as Norem writhed beneath her.

Tarn had to do something to help. The tiny dog he was holding seemed to agree. Hazel was barking madly, the collar translating the sounds as, "Mom! Mom!" over and over again. She wriggled in Tarn's hand with all her might. He couldn't tighten his grip without risking injury to her. The sound of Nancy's teeth clacking together echoed in the room, distracting Tarn. Hazel took the opportunity to wrest herself free and leap toward the ground.

He somehow managed to keep his hand underneath the tiny fur ball just enough to slow her fall. The moment the ground was in reach, she threw herself forward, scurrying toward Nancy. Tarn followed, leaping toward the pair, trying to figure out how to reach Norem without hurting Nancy or giving him the opening he needed to detonate the explosives. Nancy was putting off a haze of mist thick enough that Tarn could barely see what was happening.

Hazel let out a yelp and tumbled across the floor. Norem's thrashing had caused him to kick her. The little dog scrambled to her feet, licking her muzzle and running forward again, though her tail was tucked between her legs. Tarn felt the familiar fury rise within him. He would tear Norem apart. But first Tarn had to get Nancy off of the Tau Ceti.

The mist dissipated as Nancy looked back over her shoulder, her ears perked toward Hazel. It was all the opening Norem needed.

"Nancy, look out!" Tarn's warning was too late.

Norem yanked his arms up beneath her, his hand almost to the detonator. There was no way they could stop him in time. Tarn lurched to the side and swept Hazel up against his chest, humming the notes to increase all of her shielding to its maximum settings, as well as his own. The pup shimmied against him, but quieted as he swung himself around to half-land on Nancy's furry back. He threaded his free arm beneath her and lifted her off of Norem, leaping into the air as he did and twisting around so that Tarn's back was to the main body of the room. Heat blasted him as the explosives went off, hurling them through the air—straight toward the transit platform.

He said a silent prayer to the Maker—to any Maker who might be listening—to keep them safe as the light from the platform enveloped them all.

Chapter Thirteen

They were in blue space again. This time, Nancy didn't have the shielding from her Cygnian wristbands—or the atmosphere they could create for her. She took a tentative breath, surprised to find that she could breathe. Her nose was still filled with the scent of the explosives. Tarn's strong grip around her reassured her that he was alright. He was only holding her with one arm. Was he injured?

Her heart raced at the thought, but a wave of calm flowed to her through their bond. She felt a little wriggling body against her side and realized he was holding Hazel with his other arm. Relief coursed through her, her eyes flooding with tears. They were all okay. At least for now.

The dark cerulean and sapphire swirls of color surrounding them were punctuated with striations of silver. That was new from their last journey. The silver streaks drew closer, moving against the currents that swept them along. As they neared, they coalesced into the forms of enormous wolves, running along beside them. Tarn's grip tightened, the calm he had been projecting turning to anxiety.

"*Are these* zyln?" Nancy asked in her mind.

"*Yes,*" her *zyln* replied. "*They came through the transit portal to help us on our journey.*"

Nancy attempted to send calming emotions to Tarn, but couldn't find it within herself. Too much had happened. Too much was still going on. Nancy's mind was racing. If the *zyln* had gone through the portal to help Nancy, Tarn, and Hazel, could they also have done so for Garreth? Before Nancy had a chance to formulate her thought, the *zyln* within her reached out again.

"*Be at peace,*" it said. "*Garreth shifted when he entered blue space. He is safe and has already arrived on Ceres.*"

How long would he remain safe if the others found him there? Nancy could imagine Tobek and the others going to the transit room only to discover that Nancy, Hazel and Tarn were gone and that a Centauran in his wolf-form was there instead.

"*We have to hurry,*" Nancy thought.

"*The journey is nearly over.*"

The *zyln* at their sides pressed closer, increasing their strides. Nancy felt the currents surrounding them surge, then pull them suddenly aside. They were swept into a white light so bright it blinded her for a moment. Gravity reasserted itself. They flew off the transit platform. Tarn released her, his arms cushioning Hazel as the pair rolled to a stop. Nancy skidded on her four paws, then shook her head and quickly looked around.

As she'd feared, Tobek was there. She would never

have imagined he could look so menacing. His dark brows were drawn over his bright blue eyes, one arm raised with a blaster pointing right at her. A low growl rumbled to her side. Tobek quickly switched his target. Nancy followed the movement to see Garreth standing on the other side of the platform, his hackles raised and his muzzle low to the ground. *Zyln* soared about the room, dipping down toward Tobek, then flying back toward the ceiling.

Even worse, Peri and Cyan were also in the room. They stood on either side of Tobek, odd protrusions sticking out from their exosuits that looked suspiciously like weapons. Tobek stepped to the side, shielding Cyan from the new threat.

"I told you it was a trap," Tobek said.

"Wait," Cyan shouted. "Wait! We must understand what is happening before we take action."

"It's obvious what's happening," Tobek said. "The Centaurans are invading." He shifted his weight, his fingers tightening on the grip of his blaster.

"Tobek, stop." Nancy tried to speak, but all that came out was a drawn-out howl.

"Mom, no bark!" Hazel's familiar yapping underpinned her own speech. "No bark. No dog. Be mom."

Tarn rose to his feet unsteadily, still cradling the small dog in his arms. Was he okay? That was two trips through blue space for him. Nancy had no idea how it might affect him.

"Tarn," Tobek said. "Are you with me? Tarn?"

Tarn didn't respond. Nancy's fear grew as her soulmate looked around the room blearily. He stared at her for a moment, blinking in confusion. Nancy had to change back. She had to be able to speak to help them.

"*You must calm yourself to transform,*" her *zyln* warned.

Before she could even try, Rom sprinted into the room. His eyes widened as he saw Nancy in her wolf form, then Garreth, and finally noticed the swirling silver light of the numerous *zyln*.

"What the hell did I just walk into?" Rom said. He lifted his arms, humming notes that Nancy recognized as powering up the blaster functions in his wristbands.

"*No, no, no,*" she thought. "*This is all just a mistake. We have to stop them.*"

"*We will,*" her zyln thought back. "*Just calm yourself.*"

How could she though? Their one potential ally among the Centaurans was about to be vaporized by her friends, and she was probably next. The war would continue on, taking countless innocent lives. And something was wrong with Tarn. She could sense his confusion through their bond, see it in his oddly vacant stare.

"Tarn," Rom said. "How agro should I be getting here?" When Tarn didn't respond, Rom stepped closer. "Tarn?"

The moment Rom moved closer to Nancy, Tarn's

vision filled with purpose. He lifted his free arm, activating his own blaster function as well as a broad shield. The air in front of him rippled with a faint blue light. He turned, positioning himself between Rom and Nancy, as fierce protectiveness rolled off of him.

Nancy's eyes flooded with tears again. Whatever had happened to scramble his senses, he still knew her. He was still protecting her. They were in this together, and as long as they had each other, they could get through anything. She visualized herself taking in a deep breath and then letting it out slowly, since her body couldn't really do that in this form. Silver mist floated off of her pelt.

"They're trying to use their powers," Tobek said. "They'll freeze us where we stand."

"We are controlling the environment surrounding you," Cyan snapped. "I tell you again, you are in no danger."

Tobek's focus shifted to the *zyln* floating overhead. He did not look convinced.

Nancy pushed that out of her mind. She closed herself off to everything except Tarn. To him protecting her. To the thought of him holding her in his arms. To the nascent love growing between them as their souls recognized their other half in each other. His spine plates rose, and she felt an echo of her emotions coming back to her with increasing clarity.

He was fighting to come back to her. She wanted to be ready to wrap him in her arms when he did. Light rippled over her fur. Her arms shrank, and changed shape. She pushed herself up to stand on two legs and was delighted to find they would support her.

"Tarn?" Her voice was shaky, but the word that came out was human.

Tarn turned to look at her over his shoulder. The tightness around his eyes softened and he let out a huge breath. He shook his head, then looked back at Rom, Tobek, and the Vegans. He lowered his arm, dropping his shields and powering down his wristbands. Nancy ran to him and threw her arms around his neck. He buried his face in her shoulder, wrapping his free arm around her. Hazel whimpered and licked Nancy's cheek.

"Okay…" Tobek said. "What? I mean… What the fuck just happened there? Does somebody want to tell me what the hell is going on?"

Nancy peered out from Tarn's grip to see Garreth rise to his feet, leaving his wolf-form behind. He stared at her with his dark eyes. Nancy nodded, hoping to reassure him.

"How long has Nancy been a Centauran?" Tobek exclaimed.

"Not long." Nancy let out a laugh and wiped at the corner of her eyes, trying to dry them. "We have a lot to catch you up on."

"I'll say." Rom shook his head, but lowered his arms as well. Nancy heard the distinctive notes that deactivated his own wristbands.

"This is Garreth." Nancy gestured toward Garreth. "He's a friend." His jaw tightened, but he didn't contradict her.

"And the spooky things flying around above our heads?" Tobek prompted.

"Those are *zyln*," Nancy said. "They're another life form from the Centauran system."

"They are not from Centaurus." Peri's voice was laced with contempt.

"*You aren't?*" Nancy asked her *zyln*.

"*Not originally,*" it responded.

"*Why does he seem angry?*"

"*We... have a history with the Vegans.*"

"This is not possible," Cyan muttered. "A human cannot bond with a *zyln*. Only Centaurans can."

"It's not the first time we've done something unexpected, right?" Nancy said. "I mean, the Cygnians didn't think they could find soulmates here. Earth is full of surprises. And humans can figure out how to get along with anyone. We're really adaptable that way."

Cyan's eyes widened. Her tail began to swish back and forth behind her.

"Peri," she said, her neck curving at an odd angle as she half-crouched before him. "You do not think—"

"Shh." Peri whispered something harshly in their language. He stood straighter and said, "We will need to... to examine you. Later. Right now, we must confer."

Before she could say anything else, the pair disappeared. Literally disappeared. The air where they had been standing shimmered. Nancy narrowed her eyes, and could still see a faint outline of their forms as they turned and hurried down the hall. They had turned on their cloaks.

"Was it something I said?" Nancy sniffed, tears again filling her eyes. "I mean, what the heck was that all about?"

"I don't know." Tarn's voice was painfully gentle. "But we'll figure it out."

"Vegans can be moody." Rom was staring after them, one eyebrow raised. "Still, I'd have thought she'd examine you now, since you're all ready for it." Rom smirked and cast a quick glance down Nancy's body, then turned his back to her. He grabbed Tobek's shoulder and spun him around as well.

"What?" Nancy looked where he had and realized that yet again she was naked. "Oh, you have got to be kidding me. That's the third time today!" She glanced across the room and saw that Garreth was naked, too.

He saw her staring and shrugged. "You get used to it."

Nancy let out a laugh. Once it started, she couldn't stop. Too much had happened and too much was still going on. The laughter turned to sobs. Tarn turned her toward him and wrapped her in his embrace once more.

"Rom," Tarn said.

She felt Rom approach, his presence reassuring her more. Rom's own protectiveness echoed through her bond with Tarn. They were all linked now, to differing degrees. How would being Centauran impact her bond with the Cygnians? She wished she could ask Cyan, but apparently even after all the things the Vegan xenobiologist must have encountered in her travels through the galaxy, Nancy was the thing that sent Cyan over the edge. The thought set Nancy off again.

Tarn handed Hazel to the other Cygnian, then wrapped both arms around her, drawing her closer. His hearts beat strongly and calmly, lulling hers to a slower beat. His love for her flowed into her, filling her with warmth, bolstering her strength.

"It's alright," Tarn murmured into her ear. He nuzzled her hair. "We're safe. We're home. We'll figure everything else out in time."

"Anybody want to tell me what to do with this guy while you're figuring all that out?" Tobek said.

Nancy had to pull herself together. She could break down again later. There were still things that needed to be dealt with immediately.

"Rom, can I borrow your tunic?" she asked.

Rom smirked and nodded. "Sure."

He handed Hazel to Tarn, then pulled off his tunic and gave it to her. She quickly donned it, making the same adjustments she'd done before. It didn't take as long this time.

"I'm getting way too much practice at this," she murmured. "Tobek, can you run and get something for Garreth to wear?" Tobek glanced up at the *zyln* circling overhead. "They're fine. Seriously. The other transit room just blew up, so no one is going to be following us for a while."

"Blew up?" Tobek said, his eyebrows rising.

"We'll explain when you get back." She made a shooing gesture as if hurrying him along in his task. He grimaced, but turned and strode from the room.

"Mom," Hazel said, squirming in Tarn's arms as she sought to get to Nancy. "Mom!"

"Come here, baby." Nancy took the wriggling dog and held her close, planting kisses on her forehead.

"It won't be long till he's back," Rom said. "Better say your piece while you can."

"Was I that obvious?" Nancy said. Rom just shrugged. She turned her attention to Garreth. "Before we get into everything, I just… I want to know that you're okay."

Garreth let out a terrible sound, like a laugh that was twisted by too much pain and became more of a groan. His eyes glittered. Ice spread out from his feet, spreading over the transit platform and crawling up the walls. Hazel whimpered and burrowed deeper against Nancy's chest.

After what felt like a long time, Garreth shook his head and said, "You were right. About Norem. About the Tau

Ceti's plan."

"Norem," Rom's spine plates rose and he stiffened, the name itself instinctually preparing him for battle. Rom glanced at Nancy, but she shook her head and motioned for him to stay still.

"Everything I thought I knew was a lie," Garreth continued. "My people are being led down a terrible path, and they have no idea."

"When people you trust tell you something that makes a sort of sense to you, it's hard to know what's real and what's not," she said. She couldn't help but think of Tarn and all the things his mother had taught him. "Your people have been wronged by the High Council. But they are gone and we're all still here. We have to find a way to live together. To help each other. We have to stop this stupid war."

"It will not be so easy as that." Garreth swallowed hard, then cleared his throat. "Our leader will not wish to admit that he was duped and wrong. He will not want to believe that our allies are so barbaric. That we left—" His voice broke off and he quickly looked away, that tendon working in his jaw.

Nancy couldn't take it. She rushed forward. Garreth didn't move, he simply closed his eyes, as if resigned to whatever fate she decided for him. She threw her free arm around his shoulder and pulled him into a hug. Hazel cautiously stretched up and licked his chin, whimpering and wagging her tail.

"It's okay, new dog," Hazel said. "It's okay."

Garreth leaned his head down, pulling Nancy up against him, and buried his face in the crook of her shoulder. She felt his tears dampen her skin, freezing the moment they touched her. Tarn was behind her, not a single trace of anger or jealousy emanating through their bond. All she felt from him was sympathy and pity. He placed his hand on Garreth's shoulder, lending his own support.

Chapter Fourteen

"How could we have been so wrong?" Garreth murmured.

The Centauran's pain was as evident as the ice spreading thicker and thicker on the walls of the room. Tarn had no doubt of his remorse for what his people had done. If Tarn thought that he had been part of leaving Cygnian soulmates to such a horrific fate, he would go mad with guilt and grief. Garreth did not have that luxury. They needed him if they were going to turn this around.

"It's easy to believe people who are telling us what we think we want to hear," Nancy said. "Especially if they're giving us a reason for why terrible things happened."

Maker, his soulmate was amazing. She always seemed to know what to say, to sense when people were hurting and find the right words to soothe them. Tarn's love for her grew even stronger, watching her comfort this man who had been their adversary just a few moments ago.

"We will arrange transport for you to return to Centaurus-10," Tarn said.

"I'll take the transit portal." Garreth stepped away from Nancy and quickly ran the back of his hand across his eyes. "The *zyln* can go through and check it for me, but I doubt Norem's explosives actually damaged the mechanisms."

Some of the cloud-like entities swirled around Garreth, then swiftly flew through the transit portal, vanishing from the room. Tarn shook his head, a spike of anxiety rushing through him.

"That isn't a good idea," Tarn said. "The transit portal is still too much of an unknown to use safely."

"When you came through, you seemed confused." Nancy's concern flowed out to him, filled with warmth and something he dared to call love.

"I was," Tarn said. "My thoughts were addled. I couldn't remember where I was, why I was here, or even my name. If it hadn't been for our bond, I'm not sure I could have shaken it off as quickly as I did."

Nancy reached out to him and wrapped one arm around his waist. She rested her head against his chest. "I'm so glad you did."

Tarn wrapped his arms around her and held her close. "Garreth, it's probably best if you stay here until we can find a way to get you home."

"I'll show you where you can bunk." Rom nodded toward the open doorway. "We can track down Tobek, too. These guys are about to have company."

"What do you mean?" Nancy asked.

"I felt it when you went through the transit portal,"

Rom said. "It was like you just blinked out of existence. The rest of our prism and their soulmates felt it, too. They're on their way from Earth. Speaking of which, I should probably go explain what happened so they don't come in ready to tear the place apart."

When Rom turned to leave, Nancy released Tarn and stepped forward.

"Rom, could you watch Hazel for me?" Nancy asked. "Just for a little while?"

Rom smirked and nodded. "Sure." He reached out and took the little dog, whose tail immediately started wagging.

"Play?" Hazel said, amidst barks and yips.

"How about I take you to a little grassy area we have set up on the ship for pups to use and then you take a nap?" Rom said.

Hazel whined, but then let out a huge yawn. She nuzzled against Rom's chest and closed her eyes as he stroked her forehead. Rom cast one more grin their way, then left the room. Garreth nodded toward Nancy before following him.

"Nancy—" Before Tarn could finish his sentence she was on him. She threw her arms around his neck and pulled him down for a passionate kiss.

Tarn lifted her from her feet, his spine plates snapping up and filling the room with a low hum. Mist poured out around them, Nancy's powers asserting themselves, since it was just the two of them in the room. An odd chill swept through him—not unpleasant, but one that seemed to penetrate to his bones. She deepened the kiss, pulling his thoughts toward the feel of her skin against his, her tongue delving into his mouth, her fingers burrowing through his hair.

He reached down and undid his pants, pressing his crown against her slick wetness. She gasped as he gripped her hips and drove himself deep within her. Then she was riding him, her core clenching his shaft. She tightened her grip on his shoulders, using the leverage to increase the speed of her movements. He staggered to the nearest wall, pressing her against it so that he could match the near frenzied rocking of her hips.

Each thrust sent him closer to the edge, his hearts beating ever faster as the chill wound its way through his body. Where his nerves had been on fire before, now they were alive with a white-hot flame unlike anything he'd experienced. Her skin began to glow with a dazzling light. Tarn glanced down and saw that his was doing the same. Between their chests, a gleaming silver tether linked them, the line splitting when it reached him and going to each of his hearts.

He didn't have time to wonder about what was happening, the pulse of her body demanding his full attention. Her core clenched tighter, her body stiffening as she threw her head back and screamed his name. Her climax called him to his own, pushing him over the cliff into the ecstasy of unity. He drove himself into her, over and over again, drawing out every ounce of pleasure he could, his body alive with sensation. Finally, he slowed, then stopped as he felt her relax.

Nancy draped her arms over his shoulders and let out a contented cooing sound. Tarn chuckled, then nuzzled her neck. He brushed her hair aside to reach her skin, but paused when he noticed an unfamiliar marking there. Gleaming silver, a crescent moon made up of segments that looked like crystal arced gracefully on the nape of her neck.

Tarn pulled back and looked around. The familiar rainbows of unity hung suspended in the air, but they were joined by thousands of slivers of ice, catching and reflecting the rainbows. It was unutterably beautiful.

"Nancy." Tarn's breath puffed out in a white fog.

"Hmm?" She opened her eyes blearily. They were glowing white. As he watched, the light faded, leaving her blue eyes as bright and beautiful as always.

"Look," he said.

She blinked a few times, her lips parting in wonder as she glanced around the room. Tarn let himself slide from her so that she could stand on her own feet. He quickly righted his pants, then clasped her hand in his.

"This is more than unity," Nancy said.

"It is. There's a mark on your neck that wasn't there

before."

She turned toward him, her free hand instinctively rising to her neck. Her eyes widened as she stared at him, then she smiled.

"Let me guess," she said. "It's a crescent moon made of silver crystal."

"How did you..." His voice trailed off as he realized she was staring at the same spot on the opposite side of his own neck, as if looking at a mirror of her own marking.

Nancy's eyes became unfocused and her smile deepened. Then she laughed and shook her head.

"Apparently, bonding as Cygnian soulmates wasn't enough for us," Nancy said. "Now, we're bonded as Centauran soulmates as well."

"How is that possible?"

"My *zyln* says it's part of their way." She angled her head to the side and nodded as if listening to someone. "It can protect you now, the same as it does me. It's really happy to be learning about us."

Tarn wasn't sure how he felt about there always being a third entity with them. He hadn't considered the *zyln* when the others had left. He'd thought they were alone. But now, they would never truly be alone. He was trying to be open to the concept that Nancy was a shifter, but this whole thing with the *zyln* was hard for him to adjust to. He would have to, though. It was part of her.

"What is it?" Nancy asked.

"I just... It doesn't... I mean, when we..."

Nancy laughed. "Don't worry, it doesn't pay attention when we're doing *that*."

"But it's part of you. Permanently."

Her smile faded somewhat. "It is. And we're going to just have to get used to that. But it doesn't mean that we can't have privacy. We've come to an understanding. There are times when my *zyln* needs to sort of go dormant, and it's fine with that."

Tarn laughed.

"What?" Nancy asked.

He smiled. "You really can make friends with anyone."

She joined in with his laughter, then tilted her head up to kiss him again—a much more gentle, languid kiss than the one before. Tarn relished it, her softness, her willingness to be open with him. He would do everything in his power to be the same for her.

She was just beginning to deepen the kiss when they were interrupted by the sound of footsteps in the hall. Many footsteps.

Bron was the first one through the door. He barreled into the room, skidding to a stop in front of Tarn and immediately embracing him. Nancy stepped away to give them space.

"What happened?" Bron demanded. His blue eyes glowed with the intensity of his emotion, gleaming off of the cybernetic arm looped around Tarn's shoulders. "Are you well?"

Kral and Lar ran in behind him. Tarn was humbled by the worry on his crown prince's face, easily visible despite Kral's enormous beard and mane of sapphire hair. Even more surprising, Lar's spine plates were standing up and crackling with electricity. Both warriors approached, pulling Tarn into hugs of their own.

"You were gone," Lar said. "We couldn't sense you at all. And then when you returned to us, you were so distant. And then you disappeared again. I was certain you had gone to the Maker."

"I hope you are the only one with that honor for quite some time." Tarn angled his head to stare at Lar's enhanced spine plates sticking out from among the thick braids of his dark blue hair. "If all of us are given similar gifts from the Maker, I'm not sure the *Arrow* can handle it."

Lar laughed and clapped Tarn on the back. "I'm sure you would keep her together, as you always do."

Rom strode into the room, his cocky smile oddly absent. A deep furrow was carved between his eyebrows. Before Tarn could comment on it, two Earthlings entered with Nuar, who was hovering over his soulmate, Lian. The petite woman was scowling, her eyes glowing as red as Nuar's. The skin around them had begun to turn the same blue as her soulmate's.

"I'm not an invalid," Lian snapped. "Go check on your

friend. You're a freaking doctor, for crying out loud."

"I'm sure Tarn is fine." Another woman stepped closer as she entered the room—Lar's soulmate, Sophie. She had her long brown hair pulled up in a bun and wore a Cygnian tunic. She smiled brightly at Tarn when she saw him. "See?"

Sophie's sisters, Becca and Amy, followed after her, finding unobtrusive spots along the wall to stand and observe. Dorn, the last member of their prism, followed, standing close to his soulmate, Amy. Becca crossed her arms over her chest, casting a quick, reassuring glance at her soulmate, Kral.

"Then go check on *my* friend," Lian said. "Rom said she was with Tarn when the dumbass went through the teleportation thingy."

"I'm sure Nancy is fine." The Earthling next to Lian leaned closer and bumped their shoulders together. Her brown skin also was beginning to show undertones of sapphire and her eyes glowed blue the same as her soulmate, Bron's. Both women carried the future of the Cygnian people—they were pregnant.

Tarn's hearts felt like they were swelling in his chest. Someday, Nancy would carry his child as well. He turned to her, wanting nothing more than to draw her into his arms and never let go. Lian beat him to it.

"Oh my god, Nancy." Lian ran to her friend and threw her arms around her neck. "I was so worried."

Olivia joined the pair, rubbing her hand over Lian's back. Nancy reached out and pulled Olivia into their hug.

"I'm okay," Nancy said. "Better than okay."

Lian leaned back and said, "You and Rom hit it off?"

"Uh…" Nancy's eyes widened as she looked over at Tarn. "Not exactly."

"Where are your clothes?" Olivia asked.

"Which ones?" Nancy laughed. "It's been a ridiculously eventful night."

Had everything really transpired in just one night? Tarn could barely believe it. And yet, here he was, bonded to his Earthling soulmate. Mated to his Centauran partner. Falling more deeply in love by the moment with this amazing woman.

"You have to tell us everything," Lian said. "Did you really go through the death machine?"

"It's not a death machine." Nancy shook her head. "It's a transit platform."

"A transit platform?" Lar asked, his tone laced with surprise.

"How did you survive?" Sophie stepped forward tentatively, obviously not wanting to intrude on the trio's space. "I'm sorry for asking so bluntly, but Lar and I have seen people go through it before. Unsuccessfully."

"They didn't have this." Nancy reached up and slid the armband off of her bicep. She handed it to Sophie.

"What is it?" Sophie asked.

"It's what was in Zakarri's lockbox," Tarn said. "We think it's an activator that connects this transit platform to another on Centaurus-10."

"The Centauran homeworld?" Lar took a menacing step forward. The electricity that had infused his spine plates when his soulmate effectively brought him back from the dead crackled and sparked. Sophie reached out and rested her hand on his arm.

"Is that as bad as it sounds?" Kral asked, his voice low and level.

"It's worse." Everyone turned at the new voice. Garreth stood in the doorway, his head bowed and shoulders hunched.

Tarn felt a wave of appreciation from Nancy. She extracted herself from Olivia and Lian's hug and joined Tarn, interlacing her fingers with his. The other two Earthlings' eyebrows rose high on their foreheads.

"You and *Tarn?*" they both said at once.

"Why is that so hard to believe?" Tarn said, not bothering to hide his indignation.

"Just…" Olivia cast a quick glance at Lian. "You're so different."

"Well, opposites can attract." Nancy smiled up at him. "And if we were too similar, we wouldn't have anything to learn from each other."

He squeezed her hand gently. "And then we couldn't grow."

She laughed and leaned against him, resting her head on his arm.

"Okay, that's... adorable." Lian shuddered. Olivia bumped her shoulder against her friend's again.

Tarn turned his attention back to Garreth. The Centauran was casting brief glances around the room, not meeting anyone's eyes till his locked with Nancy's. She nodded her encouragement. Garreth looked to Tarn, who held his gaze, then nodded slowly. Garreth walked farther into the room.

"This is Garreth," Tarn said. "He is a friend." He felt Nancy's approval wash over him like a wave of warmth. "And he is Centauran."

The other Cygnians' spine plates snapped up. Tarn raised his hand in a calming gesture. "He means us no harm. He's here to help." Tarn nodded encouragement at Garreth, urging him to go on.

"Tobek showed me Norem's lab," Garreth said. "*This* Norem's lab."

"What does he mean, 'this Norem'?" Kral asked.

"Norem has been cloning himself and using the Coalition's mental programming technology to share information between all the versions he created and his original self," Tarn said.

"You are fucking kidding me," Nuar bellowed. "As if it isn't bad enough we have to deal with Zakarri. How many times are we going to have to kill this guy before we've stamped Norem out?"

"As many as it takes." Bron's voice was a low, warning rumble. Olivia walked over to him and wrapped her arms around his mechanical arm, hugging it tight.

"Guys, we need to focus," Nancy said. She turned her attention back to Garreth and continued in a soft, encouraging voice. "What did you find?"

"I believe you that my Norem was trying to link our transit platforms," Garreth said. "But it was more than that. He would question me about the *zyln* who used the transit platform to explore blue space and asked endless questions about how they could survive and what it would take for a corporeal entity to do so."

"That sounds like what this Norem was working on," Tarn said.

Garreth nodded. "I checked his files. He was trying to bioengineer soldiers capable of withstanding the trip through blue space. I believe that is why he infused Tobek and the others with Cygnian DNA."

"So, Cygnians can use the transit platform safely?" Nancy asked.

"I think so." Garreth straightened a bit. "As can Centaurans."

Everything had happened so quickly when they arrived, Tarn hadn't had a chance to marvel at that yet. But Garreth was right. The Centauran had made the journey and survived.

"You didn't have the activator," Tarn said. "Are these two transit platforms already linked now?"

"If so, we need to prepare for an invasion immediately." Dorn stepped away from the wall where he'd been leaning. "The Centaurans might not know yet that they could use the transit platform to reach the Sol system, but it's only a matter of time."

"I don't think that's how I reached this platform," Garreth said. "The *zyln* who have been traveling through blue space say that they can reach any system they wish, just as we do when using our ships' blue space engines."

"But then, you could go anywhere," Tarn said.

"What's a *zyln*?" Nuar asked.

"They're energy beings that give Centaurans their powers over cold and allow them to shift into wolf form." Tarn pointed at the wispy forms floating above them.

Dorn's spine plates rose, as did Bron's and Nuar's. The vibrations reverberated within the room.

"Don't worry, they're friends," Nancy said.

Tarn's fellow warriors didn't look convinced.

"Wait, did you say 'shift into wolf form?'" Lian's eyebrows rose, her voice laced with excitement. "Are there freaking space werewolves?"

Tarn could sense Nancy's unease. He wrapped his arm around her and pulled her closer.

"Garreth, explain." Tarn wanted to move the topic away from shifters as quickly as possible. Not because of

his own unease—which, he could barely believe, was gone
—but for Nancy's sake.

"The *zyln* haven't figured out how to return to the same
place twice," Garreth continued. "Blue space is always in
flux, and they don't have the benefit of navigational
computers. But they can always find their way home."

"How?" Dorn asked.

"They feel a pull." Garreth pinched his lips together as
if he didn't want to say more, but his eyes locked with
Nancy's, an odd longing entering his expression.

"If the pull leads you to Centaurus-10, how did you end
up on Ceres?" Kral asked.

"I…" Garreth shook his head, then stared at the floor.

"It's okay, Garreth." Nancy dropped Tarn's hand and
approached Garreth. She rested her hands on his arms and
ducked her head till their eyes met. "Remember what I
said before? Sometimes you have to be the first one to
trust. Tarn and I trust you. You can trust us and our
friends."

Garreth shook his head again, then looked up to the
ceiling. He let out a deep sigh.

"I felt a pull," Garreth said. "But it led me here.
Something in the Sol system led me here." His eyes met
Nancy's.

"Not something," she said. "Someone."

Chapter Fifteen

Garreth had a soulmate somewhere in the Sol system. Nancy was sure of it. Just as sure as she was that he would not leave the system until he found her.

"You have to help us stop this war," Nancy said.

Garreth nodded. "I will do everything in my power."

"*He understands*," Nancy's *zyln* happily thought to her. She shared the sentiment.

"Okay." She felt a broad smile stretch her face. She was sure they would find a way to convince the Centauran leader to stop the war. If they all worked together, they could help everyone. Maybe even teach the Tau Ceti to stop being such jerks.

"That's it?" Lian let out a disgusted snort. "Nancy, I know you want to believe the best about everyone and try to find the good in them—and I love that about you—but I'm not so trusting."

"His soulmate pulled him here," Nancy said, brightly. "There is no way he's going to let an invasion come to our system while she's out there."

"Oh damn," Lian said.

"What about after he finds her?" Dorn stepped closer to

Garreth, staring down at the Centauran. "Your people are extremely loyal to each other. It's hard to believe you would stand against them."

"I will stand for what I believe to be right," Garreth said, moving away from Nancy to square off with Dorn. "And 'my people' is a more expansive term than any of us realized, if it is true that all Earthlings can bond with *zyln*."

Nuar laughed. "Earthlings can bond with an energy being native to Centaurus-10? I don't think so."

Nancy didn't bother correcting him about *zyln* not being from the Centaurus system. She still needed to pry more information from the Vegans about that, once Peri and Cyan were done 'conferring.'

"All Earthlings will be considered Centaurans once our leader sees the truth of this," Garreth said.

Nuar laughed again, most of the others joining in with him, their tone mocking. Nancy's heart beat faster. The air around her and Garreth began to fill with fog. Dorn and the others lifted their arms, bracing themselves as if for battle. Bron and Nuar hurried to their soulmates, urging them behind them.

"It's true," Nancy said. "Earthlings can bond with *zyln*."

"You seem very sure of yourself," Dorn said, eyeing Nancy with an appraising stare.

"*We need them all to understand,*" Nancy thought to her *zyln*. "*Will you help me?*"

"*Always*," her *zyln* replied, a feather-light touch spreading warmth across her mind.

Nancy lifted her arm. "Just... chill out." A flurry of snowflakes flew out from her hand.

Dorn's eyes widened slightly. She heard gasps from some of the other Cygnians. Tarn came up behind her and rested his hands on her shoulders.

"Nancy—" Olivia said, edging out from behind Bron.

"Do you have ice powers?" Lian blurted, lifting Nuar's arm so she could move to stand in front of him. "Do you have ice powers *and* you're a freaking *space werewolf?*"

Nancy laughed at her friend's enthusiasm. "Yeah. I guess I'm the first Earthling-Cygnian-Centauran."

"It's true." Tarn gently squeezed her shoulders. "Rom saw her shift from her wolf form when we arrived."

Warmth and appreciation flowed into her through their bond. She couldn't sense any misgivings at all. Only acceptance and love. Her eyes filled with tears and she quickly blinked them away. She leaned back against his chest as he wrapped his arms around her.

"We believe you, brother," Kral said. "It's just... quite a bit to process."

"What is there to process?" Lian's eyes were wide, a huge grin crossing her face. "This is the coolest thing ever! Nancy—"

"I am not going to shift for you," Nancy said. "Not until Garreth has helped us fabricate some outfits that won't be destroyed every time I do so." Her eyes widened, excitement replacing her doubts from a moment before. "Oh my god. I get to design a whole new wardrobe."

"I want to be a space werewolf, too," Lian yelled. She looked up at the misty life forms circling above their heads and actually reached one arm up.

"Don't even think about it," Nancy snapped. "Your body is going through enough changes with the baby."

Lian pouted, but lowered her arm. Nuar wasn't laughing anymore. He inched closer to his soulmate, staring warily at the *zyln* lurking above.

"Will I still be able to bear children?" Nancy hadn't thought of it before, but seeing Lian, the question filled her mind. She wanted to have children with Tarn.

"Of course," her *zyln* thought back. *"Shifting form has never hurt a Centauran child. And if you are concerned, I can help you maintain this form whenever you are carrying a child."*

Her *zyln's* confidence reassured Nancy more than anything else. She especially appreciated the 'whenever you are carrying a child' part. As if it would happen more than once.

"Thank you," Nancy thought.

She turned in Tarn's embrace and wrapped her arms around his chest, burying her face against the strength of him.

"Everything's going to be okay," she said.

"I know." Tarn leaned down and kissed her gently. His love flowed through her, a warmth unlike anything she'd experienced, even when they bonded, flooding her soul as she let herself sink into him, her soulmate.

"We have more to discuss." Dorn's voice cut into the moment. Tarn and Nancy broke off the kiss.

"Of course," Nancy said, though she kept her arms around Tarn. "Sorry about that."

"There is never a need to apologize for bonding with your soulmate." Lar had his arms around Sophie, who was leaning her head against his chest and smiling at Tarn and Nancy.

As Nancy looked around the room, she saw that most of the Cygnians and their soulmates had paired up in a similar manner. Even Becca and Kral stood shoulder-to-shoulder, their fingers interlaced as they held hands. Only Rom and Garreth stood alone. Nancy's heart went out to them—especially Rom, after what he'd confessed to her earlier. At least Garreth knew that his soulmate was somewhere in the Sol system. Rom didn't know if his even existed.

Rom stood with his head bowed, his hair falling in front of his face. Nancy could see the violet glow of his eyes, the tension in his shoulders as he held himself as still as a statue. The only part of him that moved was his spine plates, which vibrated strongly along his back.

"Does it have to be a soulmate?" Amy, the youngest of

the Myers sisters, spoke up.

Garreth looked grateful for the chance to switch topics. "What do you mean?"

"Could you key in on someone else?" Amy said.

"There was mention of a project." Garreth nodded, staring thoughtfully at the ground for a few moments. "MIN-D. I didn't read too much of it, because it seemed so ludicrous."

"Indulge our curiosity," Lar said.

"There was something about Earthlings—all Earthlings, not just humans—that fascinated Norem." Garreth looked over at Nancy. "I'm beginning to share the sentiment."

"Well, you and Cyan can exchange notes." Nancy tried to tone down the hint of bitterness to her voice. "She freaked out that I could bond with a Cygnian and a *zyln*. She and Peri are 'conferring' somewhere."

"The adaptability of humans is truly extraordinary," Nuar said. He smiled at Lian and said, "For which I am eternally grateful."

Lian actually smiled back and let him pull her into a hug. Nancy wanted to bask in the moment, but Amy was determined to keep them on task.

"How did the MIN-D project relate to all this?" Amy asked.

Garreth's brow furrowed. "Norem's notes on the topic were obscure, but he was trying to create a psychic link between humans and animals. Specifically, dogs. The project held as much importance for him as the bioengineered soldiers."

"Norem was keeping a dog in his office," Sophie said, in a grave voice.

"He was also keeping Hayley," Amy said.

Sophie winced and reached over to clasp her hand around a bracelet gleaming on her arm. "He *is* keeping Hayley. She's still alive."

"I know." Amy's voice softened. "I know. That's why this is so important. Can I see that?"

Sophie glanced at her wrist. She was wearing two charm bracelets. She took off one and handed it to Amy.

"You're sure this one is Hayley's?" Amy asked. "Not yours?"

"Hers has the BFF charm that's bent." Sophie sniffed. "Where she used it to try to pry open the panel in her cell."

Lar wrapped his arms around Sophie and pulled her against his chest. A tear rolled down her cheek that she didn't bother trying to wipe away.

Nancy only had vague information about Hayley. Olivia and Lian didn't know that much and barely talked about it. All they knew was that she was like family to the Myers sisters—Becca, Sophie, and Amy—and that Zakarri had abducted Hayley. Somehow, Norem had gotten his hands on her and no one knew where she was now. After everything Nancy had learned about Norem... Her stomach flooded with ice, thinking about his experiments. What had he done to her? What was he *still* doing?

"What are you thinking?" Dorn asked, eyeing his soulmate thoughtfully.

"I'm thinking that we're desperate and we just got our first lead." Amy held up the bracelet. "On Earth, some people believe you can detect vibrations in jewelry that people have worn for a long time."

"Don't get Sophie's hopes up with that bullshit," Becca snapped.

"Bullshit is all we have," Amy said. "Besides, look around you. Our lives are a freaking science fiction novel. Aliens? Soulmates? Space werewolves?" She gestured toward the *zyln* who were still flying above them rather than Nancy and Garreth. Somehow, it made Nancy like Amy more.

"Hayley has worn this bracelet since she was a little kid," Amy continued. "If there is any chance whatsoever that we can use it to key in on wherever she might be and use the transit portal to find her, we have to take it."

"Even if we could, who would go through?" Nuar frowned deeply. His hands were clenched into fists at his sides. "Bron and I must stay with our soulmates."

"I will," a chorus of voices said—all of the Myers sisters, as well as their mates.

"Sophie and I must go," Lar said. "We have been touched by the Maker. Our special abilities will give us an advantage."

"We have no idea how your powers will be affected by direct contact with blue space," Bron said. "Especially Sophie's."

"Hayley is my best friend," Sophie said. "I'm going."

"*She must not.*" Nancy's *zyln* thought-spoke with more urgency than she'd ever heard. "*That one is changed. Her energy is attuned to blue space. If she goes in, she will not come out.*"

"Okay, Sophie can't go." Nancy stepped forward, her arms raised as if to block Sophie from the transit platform. Everyone turned and stared at her. She swallowed nervously, then waved. "Um, hi. I'm Nancy. Space-werewolf-Cygnian." She gave a little curtsy. "I know we haven't met before, but my *zyln* says it's way too dangerous for you to jump into blue space. You won't be able to return."

"But..." Sophie stammered, a crackling sound coming from her back. "No offense, but I don't even know you."

"Sophie," Lar said gently. He reached out and stroked her arm. She half-turned toward him, revealing a row of spine plates sticking out from her back that were made out of what looked like tiny lightning bolts.

"Whoa, that is so cool." Nancy stepped forward, craning her head for a better look. When Sophie turned back toward her, she straightened suddenly. "Sorry. That is... really cool though. I'm sorry that you can't go. If it were Lian or Olivia, I don't know what I'd do if I couldn't go after them but..." Nancy's eyes widened and she smiled. "But I can go instead. Tarn and I can."

She turned back to look at him. She felt his unease, his desire to keep her safe, and her smile softened.

"Tarn, come on," Nancy said, extending her hand toward him. He took it reflexively, though he didn't move toward the platform. "We can do this."

"We don't even know how to zero in on Hayley," Tarn said. "And it's too dangerous for you to go. Let me do it myself."

She laughed and shook her head. "We're linked. Double-bonded. If we go together, we can look out for each other.

Tarn remained unconvinced. "We don't know what will happen."

Her smile softened. "We do know. Wherever we end up, we'll be fine."

"How can you be so sure of that?" he asked.

She stepped closer. "Because we'll be together."

"Dorn and I will come, too," Amy said. "I'll join with a *zyln* and—"

To his credit, Dorn didn't say anything. He sucked in a breath, but held it, glaring at Amy with glowing green eyes.

"You might want to stick a pin in the whole 'becoming a space-werewolf thing,'" Nancy said. "At least, until after the baby comes."

"Baby?" Amy said, for the first time looking anxious. "What baby?"

"Oh." Nancy made a face and looked at Dorn. "You guys didn't know yet? I guess it's my space werewolf senses..."

Dorn's eyes widened and his jaw dropped. "Nuar," he shouted.

Nuar hurried over and struck his wristbands together, quickly scanning Amy. He shook his head, but then suddenly gasped. "Maker, she's right. It's so early, but it's there." He turned to look at Nancy. "How did you know?"

"Her eyes." Nancy pointed at Amy. "There are these little green sparks in them."

Dorn and Nuar both leaned forward and stared at Amy's eyes.

"Do you see them?" Nuar asked.

"I see nothing." Dorn grasped Amy's face in his hands. "Except my fearsome soulmate." He pulled her in for a deep kiss that had Nancy blushing.

Becca put an end to it. "Knock it off. That's my baby sister."

Dorn broke off the kiss, but kept an arm protectively around Amy. Becca scrunched up her face, then suddenly burst out crying. She ran over to Amy and pulled her into an embrace. Sophie was right behind her. The sisters hugged and cried, smiling and laughing as they whispered to each other.

"Well, see?" Nancy said. "They're not going to want to leave their baby sister when she's in this condition. As soon as we figure out how to use the bracelet to find Hayley, it has to be us."

"No, it doesn't." Before Nancy could even register what was happening, Rom stepped forward and grabbed something dangling from Amy's hand.

"Rom, wait," Tarn shouted. But it was too late.

With one mighty leap, Rom cleared the twenty feet between himself and the transit platform. A brilliant flash of light blinded Nancy momentarily. Blinking, she stared around the room.

Rom was gone.

Chapter Sixteen

The blankness of Rom's disappearance tore through Tarn's hearts. Where they had been a complete prism before, now they were diminished. Rom's absence was a wound deep within him unlike anything Tarn had ever felt before. His mind reeled, his hearts pounding painfully in his chest.

Was this what the others had felt when he had gone into blue space? Not once, but twice? Tarn couldn't believe he had put his brothers through this.

"Kral, no!" Becca screamed across the room as Kral barreled toward the transit platform. Lar grabbed Kral's arm and dragged him back.

"We cannot risk you," Lar yelled. "You are the crown prince of Cygnus-Prime."

"He is my brother," Kral snarled, writhing in Lar's grip.

"He is brother to us all," Lar said.

"Someone has to go after him," Nuar said.

"We can." Tarn nodded toward Nancy.

"Wait." She grasped his arm tightly. Her eyes became unfocused and she arched her neck to look up at the *zyln*.

"Go," Garreth yelled, pointing at the transit platform. The swirling white entities flowed down toward the transit platform, initiating their own small bursts of light as they vanished.

"Will they be able to track him?" Tarn asked.

Garreth shook his head. "They will do what they can."

"It's not enough," Kral said. "We must—"

"We must think." Lar pulled Kral closer, half-embracing him. "There is too much at stake for any more of us to act rashly."

"Why would he do that?" Sophie said. "Why would he jump through the portal?"

"We were making a plan." Amy sounded angry more than anything. "We hadn't even had a chance to see if we could connect the charm bracelet to Hayley's location, but…"

"He took it." Sophie shook her head, her tears flowing anew. "Why would he take it? It's all I had left of her."

"He knew what he was doing." Nancy's voice was surprisingly calm. Tarn could sense her dread as everyone turned to her. Her eyes glimmered and she half-shrugged. She tried to smile, but it was a broken look. "We all have soulmates already. Even Garreth senses someone here. But Rom…"

"Rom just hasn't found her yet," Nuar said. "He only had to wait until—"

"He didn't feel her," Nancy broke in. "He told me

yesterday. God, was it only yesterday?" She shook her head. "You all felt your soulmates even before you came to the Sol system. But Rom never did. He thinks she hasn't been born yet. Or maybe, if she was human…"

"Maybe she died," Dorn said, his gaze intent on Amy.

"Why wouldn't he tell us this?" Lar spoke almost as if he were talking to himself. Nancy answered him anyway.

"Because he wanted you to be happy." She gestured at everyone in the room. "All of you. All of us."

"We cannot be happy if our brother is lost," Lar said. His spine plates crackled with lightning.

Tarn felt his own vibrating rapidly. Every Cygnian in the room stood ready for battle, ready to act, ready to do anything to help their prism-mate. Sophie stepped away from her sisters as her own spine plates surged to life, sparks flaring out from them and fizzing on the floor.

"There has to be a way for us to help him," Sophie said. "He's doing this to try to find Hayley for us. He doesn't even know her."

"Calm down." Amy stepped forward. "We need to think."

"Can we communicate with the *zyln* while they're in blue space?" Dorn asked.

"Only Nancy's and my *zylns* can communicate with them, and that only works when they're in the same room," Garreth said.

"So, we have to wait for them to get back to find out

what's going on." Nancy's disappointment was as clear on her face as through their bond.

"Sophie has reached through blue space before and affected people," Becca said. "Maybe we can establish a link to Rom through his wristbands and she can help guide him to a safe destination where we can meet him."

"He might be using his wristbands to keep himself safe," Bron said. "They may not have sufficient energy to respond. If he tries, it may deplete their reserves."

"Did he even bring up his shields before he entered the transit portal?" Nuar said.

Bron turned to Tarn and said, "You're the only one of us who has been through blue space. What can you tell us about it?"

"I sensed it as a void," Tarn said. "But it is chaotic. Ever in motion. My shields helped keep my body safe, but when we returned here the second time, my mind was not clear when I arrived."

"So, we can wait for the *zyln* to return and ask them how things went," Becca said. "Or we can try to contact Rom while he's in blue space and risk running down his wristbands' batteries."

Everyone was silent for a few moments. Becca crossed over to Kral and threaded her arms around his chest, pulling him close for a hug. He folded her into his embrace, resting his forehead on the top of her head.

"It's been a long time," Dorn said.

"Longer than either of Tarn's trips." Bron pulled Olivia into an embrace.

"How long do we wait before we try one of our plans?" Nuar looked around the room. No one replied, but Lian stepped closer and nestled against his chest. He gratefully drew her closer.

"It's going to be okay," Nancy murmured, her eyes closed. "It's going to be okay. We just have to believe in him. He can do this."

"You really think he can find Hayley?" Sophie was standing next to Lar, holding his hand tight.

"I think he thought so," Nancy said. "Or else he wouldn't have gone through the platform."

Tarn draped his arm over Nancy's shoulders, pulling her close. He let her faith flow through him, willing himself to share her optimism. Rom was a Cygnian warrior. No matter what else happened, he would survive this. They would reach him and bring him home.

"We should get to the *Arrow*," Tarn said. "And prepare to follow wherever Rom has gone."

"Agreed." Kral turned to Garreth. "Tarn says you are his friend. I will trust you as such."

Garreth stood straighter and nodded. "Thank you."

"Go and tell Tobek and the others what has happened," Kral said. "It will be up to them and the Vegans to protect this base and to watch for Rom's return."

"It will be done." Garreth turned and hurried from the

room.

"We cannot wait here," Kral said. "If we're going to believe that Rom will find Hayley, we need to be ready to assist him." Kral strode from the room, Becca at his side. Everyone fell in step behind them.

"Bron, I'll need you to pilot the *Arrow* until Rom returns," Kral said.

Bron nodded. "Of course."

"Lar, you'll need to manage our scans," Kral said. "I especially want you on communications, listening for any signs of Rom's arrival anywhere in the galaxy. Check systems you normally would not listen in on. If there is even a rumor of his appearance, I want us there."

"Agreed," Lar said.

"I'll help with that." Dorn increased his stride for a moment, then fell back to walk closer to Amy. She glared up at him, but then smiled.

"We all can." Becca gestured toward her sisters. "If it's something as simple as listening in on communications or parsing through data, let us help."

"Alright." Kral turned to Nuar. "You must keep our soulmates and their children safe. Check on Amy as soon as we reach the ship."

"But—" Amy began.

"I will accept no arguments on this," Kral said. "You also now hold the future of our people within you. Rom would agree that takes priority over anything else."

Amy scowled, but then her gaze became unfocused. Her hand went to her belly briefly. Dorn rested his hand on her back and she smiled up at him. Nancy reached over and grasped Tarn's hand, interlacing their fingers. Her tender smile was enough to soothe some of the ache in his hearts.

"Nancy can help with monitoring data streams as well," Tarn said. She nodded her agreement. "She can do so from engineering with me."

"As long as she doesn't distract you from the engines," Kral said.

Tarn's spine plates were still up, but his quip had them vibrating even more strongly. Before he could complain, Becca jumped in.

"You guys have only been bonded for a short time," Becca said. "There are… temptations that might surprise you with their intensity."

Nancy let out a little laugh. "Yeah, that's a good point. I promise, we'll stay focused."

Tarn squeezed her hand, hoping to comfort as much as to gain comfort himself. A short time later, they were all on the ship, heading to their respective assignments. Hazel was asleep in one of the soft dog beds they had added beneath the benches that lined the walls of the common room. Nancy checked on her briefly before following Tarn to engineering. It occurred to him that with all that had happened, she hadn't slept or eaten in a long time. He hurried to a fabricator and programmed a meal for them to share, then brought it over to her.

"It tastes better than it looks," Tarn said. "Sophie in particular has been helping Bron and me to program the ship to create meals more palatable to Earthlings."

"Well then, I am grateful to Sophie, because I am starving!" Nancy picked up a pale green cube and popped it into her mouth. Her brow furrowed as she began to chew, but then she nodded. "That's... nice, I guess. Kind of like kiwi."

She ate a bit more under Tarn's watchful gaze. There was something he was forgetting. Something humans needed that Cygnians didn't.

"Water," he said suddenly. "You need water."

"Water would be good." She smiled at him as he handed her the tray of food and hurried back to the fabricator. When he returned with a tall plastic tumbler, she emptied it in several long swallows.

"Oh my god, that tastes so good," she said. "I don't think I've ever been so thirsty."

"Do you need sleep?" Tarn took her dishes and set them aside, then gestured at the hammock which had been slung high in one corner of the engineering bay. "I can help you up to my hammock."

As soon as he spoke, images of holding her in his arms flooded his mind. He would let her sleep for a bit, then wake her with kisses and—

"Whoa." Nancy laughed, a rosy flush gracing her cheeks. "I think we just hit some of those temptations Becca warned us about. I don't need to sleep, though. I think my *zyln* is giving me extra energy."

Remembering the energy being that now inhabited his soulmate chased away his errant fantasy.

"We should have Nuar examine you as well," Tarn said.

"I'm fine. But yeah, we can do that later."

A wave of unease and sadness flowed out from her. Tarn gently ran his hands along her arms.

"What is it?" he asked.

"I just wish that Cyan had checked me over. It still weirds me out that she was so... weirded out."

"Everything will be fine."

"I like the optimism." She smiled and angled herself closer. "But how do you know that?"

"Because we're together. And as you said, if we're together, we can work anything out."

He leaned down to kiss her when a sudden wave of confusion and anxiety rocked through him. Swaying on his feet, he found himself leaning on Nancy for support. His spine plates sprang up, their vibrations somehow intense enough to cause a brief rainbow refraction in the air surrounding them. How could he create the beauty of unity when he hadn't even mated with his soulmate?

"Tarn?" she said. "Tarn, what is it?"

"It's Rom."

"Is he okay?"

"He found her."

"He found her?" Nancy's confusion gave way to excitement and hope. "Hayley?"

Tarn shook his head. "His soulmate."

Epilogue

Peri paced the small room where Cyan had set up her own laboratory. He had pieced it together for her using whatever equipment he could find in Norem's base. Now, she was hunched over a compact subatomic accelerator, studying the display screen he had designed for it with goggles formed by her exosuit that would further magnify what she could see.

It had been too long. Surely, she would have found something by now if they had reason to worry.

"Your pacing will not speed the process," she said.

"I am aware. However, I need something to do and there are few alternatives at the moment." He paused, then hurried closer. "Do you need me to modify the accelerator? I can attempt to improve its abilities to analyze even smaller particles. I was somewhat limited by the raw materials available to—"

"It is quite sufficient." Cyan straightened, the glasses her exosuit had created withdrawing from around her eyes. The nanites flowed like liquid down her neck and reformed into their usual band at that location, solidifying back into her exosuit. She folded her hands in front of her and looked at the floor, her lips pulled into a deep frown and her breathing shallow.

"Cyan..." Peri said. He lifted her hands in his. "Whatever you have found, we will face it together."

"It is as we feared. I have analyzed every sample of Earthling DNA I had available, from the simplest life forms to humans themselves. They all share the same structure. I did not find it before because I did not delve deeply enough. I did not think I needed to."

"It is not—"

"It is." Cyan finally met his eyes. Her pupils were the tiniest slits in an ocean of gold. "Adaptogenic. Earth is a repository for... for *them*."

He pulled her to her feet, resting his forehead against hers. She trembled, and he reached around with his tail to curl it around hers and hold her closer.

"They will return to Earth," she said. "They will find us here and they will punish us."

Peri did not know what to say to comfort her. The words she spoke were true.

"We must tell the others," he said.

She shook her head, though she kept it pressed against his. "The elders will make us leave. We will be doomed to roam the galaxy once more. Lost."

"Perhaps our leaders will decide to make a stand here. We have allies now."

"Will they stand with us when they learn what we have

done?"

He did not have an answer for that.

"Peri, Earth is my home," she said. "I do not wish to leave."

"Then we will stay, even if the other Vegans go."

"They will not let us."

"They will have to." He forced a smile and said, "If they choose to leave, we will confess our crimes. Once we are exiled, we can go or stay wherever we wish."

"Peri," she chided, but her lips curled up as she forced a faint smile.

"I will stay with you." He reached up and rested his hand against her cheek—a gesture he had seen countless other sentients do with someone they cared for. Someone they loved. "No matter where the stars take us, I will be at your side."

She hissed in a breath, her tail tightening around his.

"No matter where the stars take us, I will be at your side," she said.

This time, her smile was true.

—

Thank you so much for reading *Tarn: A Scifi Alien Warriors Romance*! There are so many questions answered in Tarn's book—and even more new ones asked. We have one final adventure with this band of Cygnian warriors and their fiery mates in this series, but don't worry! There is so much in store for them and everyone else you've come to know and love in the *Department of Homeworld Security* universe. Read on for a peek at the final book in the *Cygnian 7* series, *Rom: A Scifi Alien Warriors Romance!*

Rom: A Scifi Alien Warriors Romance

Cygnian 7
Book Seven

Chapter One

Warm water dripped from Hayley's chin. Her head was pounding and the small shower cubicle seemed to spin. She leaned against the cold metal wall, letting the water rinse away the last vestiges of the soap she had used to get the disgusting tank fluid out of her hair and off her body.

"Hurry up in there."

She jumped at the brusque voice of the guard stationed outside. As quickly as she could, she finished rinsing, then turned off the water. Warm air blasted her from all sides, drying her quickly. Even her hair was left only a little damp. The artificial breeze ended and Hayley stepped outside, resting her hand on the wall to stay upright.

Why was everything spinning? Her joints ached as if she'd never used them before, her eyes barely able to focus. She felt oddly disconnected from the pain. Nothing felt real.

She couldn't show weakness. Couldn't show anything at all. Nothing out of the ordinary, even though there was nothing ordinary about her life at all.

She had been abducted. Twice. Once by a shapeshifting mercenary who had promised to protect her, but left her with someone so much worse. Someone who had taken her far from her homeworld. Who was using her for experiments that she didn't understand, but knew she had to do everything in her power to thwart.

Normal... Normal. Everything is normal.

Because when it wasn't normal, that caught his attention. Norem's.

She shuddered, forcing herself to walk the short distance between herself and the pile of clothes waiting for her. White panties, white sports bra, gray jumpsuit. The only clothing she'd seen in… How long had it been? She'd lost track. Her memory was foggy. Even worse than usual.

Sophie. Amy. Becca. Buddy. David. Shannon.

She went through the names of her family back home. Her foster-family. They had befriended her family when her mother was dying of cancer, then they had taken her in when her grandma died a decade later. Hayley had only been seventeen. Now, she and the Myers sisters, Becca, Amy, and Hayley's best friend, Sophie, all lived in Hayley's family home.

Someday, she would see it again. Someday, she would see *them* again.

She had a new family now. People she needed to help, that she *could* get back to.

As quickly as she could, she dressed, then stepped out into the corridor beyond the cleansing chamber. The Tau Ceti guard was waiting for her, wearing his form-fitting dark brown uniform. Three arcs of bronze metal curved over each shoulder and a matching bronze belt wrapped around his waist. A ray-gun was strapped to it. She knew better than to make a grab for it. These guys might look like something out of a cheesy, old-fashioned sci-fi movie, but they were fast and deadly.

He glared at her until she turned and started down the corridor. At least he didn't seem to find it odd that she was hunched over and walking slowly. Her equilibrium still felt off. Norem would undoubtedly want to know that. It was probably a side-effect of whatever his most recent experiment on her had been. Mercifully, she couldn't remember what it was. She must have been unconscious for it.

A flash of memory assailed her. Bubbles bursting from her mouth as the breathing apparatus that sealed most of it and trailed down into her lungs was pulled out. Blue and green lights searing her eyes. Her skin burning and itching like she was sunburned bad enough to peel.

"Keep moving."

The guard shoved her and she almost fell. She hadn't even realized that she had stopped to lean against the wall. What was wrong with her? This wasn't like the other treatments. Was it?

Her memory was so blurry, like looking out through the liquid in her tank. Looking out at Norem, his long face distorted through the viscous fluid. His smile...

She shuddered again, but kept moving down the hall. Left foot, right foot. Left foot, right foot. Strangely, her left ankle and knee didn't ache like the rest of her. She used that to help her limp along down the corridor. The plain metal hall seemed to stretch on forever. Hayley wondered if she would ever see anything else. Finally, she arrived at the door to her cell. It slid open without a sound. She stumbled inside, barely making it to her bed before she collapsed.

There was no escape. Not even in her sleep. Dreams assailed her. Swaths of blue swirling in maddening circles. Cobalt and sapphire with streaks of silver that flew around her like ghosts.

"Hayley? Hayley?"

A soft voice edged around the corners of her mind. A voice of caring and love. The only comfort she would get in this hell.

"Where are you? I can't hear you anymore."

"Mindy?"

Even though Hayley couldn't see her friend, she could feel the huge dog wagging her tail happily.

"Hayley! Where did you go? You were gone for so long..."

"I'm sorry, Mindy. I... I don't know where I was."

Hayley did her best to shield Mindy from what had actually happened. She always did. The one blessing in this place was that Norem treated Mindy well. Hayley didn't want to risk that by letting him know that his project was much more successful than he had imagined.

Norem wanted to connect Hayley and Mindy so that they could use each other as beacons in some kind of... teleportation experiment or something. Hayley only knew that much because Norem spoke freely in front of Mindy, not realizing how much the dog understood—or that she could communicate everything he said to Hayley telepathically. Hayley was sure Mindy's intelligence was beyond anything Norem had expected. So was their bond.

"You feel different," Mindy thought.

"Different how?"

"I don't know. New."

New? Hayley didn't feel new. She felt ancient. Worn. Exhausted. She rolled over on the bed and stared at the plain bronze ceiling.

"Rest now," Mindy thought.

"Okay. You, too."

Hayley was only just starting to doze when a voice sounded over the speakers in her cell. This one was welcome.

"Hey, stranger."

Hayley smiled despite everything. Tears flooded her eyes as relief coursed through her.

"Katie?"

"The one and only." After a pause, Katie said, "You were gone for a long while that time. You okay?"

"I'm great. Just like going to the spa."

Neither of them liked to talk about the tank. They had come up with their own little code words, trying to maintain their sanity through their absolutely insane circumstances.

"There was a hubbub while you were gone," Katie said. "Some sort of big transfer. I couldn't get details. Slime-o was absolutely paranoid about it and didn't put anything in the computers."

Hayley shuddered, even with Katie using their nickname for Norem. Another thing they had learned in their captivity was that the Tau Ceti had evolved from something akin to a frog. Cannibalistic frogs who ate the rest of their broodmates once they hatched, 'leaving only the strongest to survive.'

"You still with me, Hayley?" Katie asked.

"Yeah, sorry. This last round really wore me out."

"You know, it's funny," Katie said after a few moments of silence. "You were gone so long, I thought maybe this time you weren't coming back."

"No way. You know our deal. We get out of here together."

"We get out of here together. Plus the dog." Katie laughed.

"Plus the dog." Hayley chuckled as well. "I'm just glad Slime-o hasn't brought in any new prisoners that we'll need to rescue when we make our great escape."

Katie was silent for a while again.

"Katie?"

"Yeah, about that... I was digging through the files again with these handy, freakish abilities that Slime-o managed to impart."

Whatever Norem had done to Katie had given her the ability to sort of project her mind into the station's computer systems. She was also a whiz with technology, though neither of them had access to anything remotely useful when they weren't under close scrutiny. Katie had been careful to hide most of her abilities from Norem— like the fact that she could secretly communicate with Hayley through the station's intercom system. Katie had shared just enough of what she could do to keep her project 'active.' Neither of them knew what happened to the women who were part of projects that ended. All they knew was that they never saw them again.

"Please tell me he isn't bringing some other poor soul to this hellscape," Hayley said.

"I'm not sure. There's mention of a new subject, but I'm not finding any new files. I don't understand it."

"I'd worry about you more if you did. Slime-o's mind remains a mystery."

"I guess that means the telepathy project he's working on with you is still a no-go?"

"Yeah. Yeah, that's a no-go." Hayley hated keeping secrets from Katie, but even with everything they'd been through, she wasn't sure who to trust—aside from Mindy.

Hayley closed her eyes and covered them with her arm, trying to block out the lights. She still saw sparks. Was she getting a migraine? Great, that was just what she needed.

"I think I need to get some sleep," Hayley said. "Do you mind if we talk more later?"

"Not at all. I just... I missed you."

"I missed you, too." At least, Hayley was certain she would have, if she'd been conscious for the experiments. She wondered what Norem had done to her this time. A shiver went down her spine. Best not to think of it.

A short burst of static let Hayley know that Katie had disconnected their cells. Even though Katie's technokinetic abilities would probably be more handy in an escape attempt, Hayley was grateful for the telepathy that Norem had somehow activated. It wasn't just that she wasn't alone, but that she could be there for Mindy. She only wished she could see her in person and give her a big hug. Norem might be kind to the dog, but he wasn't the most affectionate guy. Mostly because Mindy kept biting him. She was a good judge of character.

Lights flashed against the backs of Hayley's eyelids again. She covered her eyes with both hands, but the light kept coming, each burst closer than the last. She sat up and leaned her elbows on her knees, blinking quickly. The lights kept flashing.

Hayley stared around her small cell, unsure of what she was seeing. A line of white light had appeared, hovering in the middle of the small room. She scrambled farther back on the bed, but it was bracketed against the wall. There was nowhere for her to run to. Nowhere to hide.

The line of light expanded like a seam opening. Within, swirls of blue twisted around in mesmerizing patterns. Hayley leaned forward, almost willing to just jump through and see if it led to freedom. But then she thought of Mindy and Katie. She couldn't leave them behind.

A silhouette formed before her—a lighter blue that didn't swirl like the rest. It grew larger or closer. Hayley couldn't tell. All she could tell was that it was a man. He suddenly fell forward into the room. The light flashed once more, then vanished.

Hayley sat frozen on her bed, her chest heaving and her heart racing. The man was crouching in front of her, wearing eggshell-white pants and matching boots. And that was it, aside from a pair of chrome wristbands that covered a few inches of his forearms. A long row of serrated spines ran down the center of his back, like a stegosaurus, only dark blue. His skin was a lighter shade, as was the long hair that fell in front of his face, obscuring her view of his features. Beneath him, a pool of violet light illuminated the floor like the beam of a flashlight.

"He... hello?" Hayley said. "Are you okay?"

His dinosaur spine plates stiffened, rising till they were standing straight up on his back. They began to flutter, then vibrate, blurring like the wings of a hummingbird. They even let out a low humming noise. It filled the room, washing over her skin and seeping in through tired muscles and aching joints. The vibration relaxed her, eased her pain, made her feel... real somehow.

Tingles spread up and down her spine, spreading out along her arms and legs. She felt her cheeks heat as other areas also heated, molten desire pooling deep in her belly. The man slowly uncurled, the muscles of his back rippling as he straightened up and up and up. His head almost brushed the ceiling of her cell. He must be pushing seven feet tall. Her jaw dropped as he shook his head, flipping his hair out of his face.

He was unutterably gorgeous.

Square jaw, strong cheekbones, straight nose, and dark eyebrows over glowing violet eyes. His hair brushed his massive shoulders. His arms were corded, his chest and shoulders broad. Rows of abs were stacked on top of each other on his abdomen. He was absolutely ripped. His waist tapered, then flared out to narrow hips. She could clearly see the outline of his muscled legs through his pants.

She had died. She must have. Men this perfect did not exist in reality. And even if they did, she certainly wouldn't react with so much lust and... longing for them.

"*Hayley?*" Mindy's voice suddenly appeared in Hayley's mind. "*Are you okay?*"

"*I am,*" she thought back, carefully walling off the feelings the man was generating within her from Mindy. "*I think I am.*"

"*You're more there.*"

"*What?*"

"*You're... more Hayley. More there. It's good.*"

"*I'm sorry, Mindy, I don't understand.*"

She heard a whining sound in her mind. Mindy didn't know how to explain better.

"*Don't worry,*" Hayley thought.

"*Someone is there.*"

Hayley didn't want to scare Mindy, but at the same time, if the dog could sense this guy, maybe she could help Hayley figure out if he was friend or foe.

Who was Hayley kidding? He had appeared out of some kind of tear in the space-time continuum. He probably wanted to abduct Hayley again. Looking him up and down, she wasn't sure she'd object this time.

Especially if there were no experiments involved. But he would have to take Mindy and Katie along, too.

"Can you read his mind?" Hayley thought.

"He's confused. It's all... blue. But I like him."

That was enough for Hayley to get her racing heart under control. Her dizziness seemed to have left and she realized she felt better than she had a moment before. Her spine was tingling weirdly, but of all the side-effects of Norem's experiments, that was nothing. Encouraged, she decided to be the one to make the first move.

"Hi," she said.

He angled his head to the side as if he hadn't understood her. Did he not have whatever universal translator everyone seemed to use out here in space? He shook his head, weaving on his feet suddenly.

"Are you okay?" she asked.

He managed to steady himself. She noticed that he kept one fist closed. Not in a threatening way, but as if he was holding something. He looked at it, then back to her.

"Who are you?" she asked.

He blinked a few times, the glow in his eyes fading till all she saw was their lovely violet hue. In a rich voice that sent tingles down her spine, he said, "Hayley?"

Her stomach felt like it dropped through the floor. How did he know her name? He had to be working with Norem. What was his game, though? What did he want? She tried to keep herself frozen, not revealing any of her distress, but he seemed to see it anyway.

"I won't hurt you," he said. "I would never hurt you."

"Who are you?"

"I… I don't know."

"You know my name, but not your own?"

This had to be a trick. He was trying to get her to trust him. To reveal the secrets Norem undoubtedly suspected she was keeping. She wouldn't fall for it, even though the idea of having this huge, strong protector made her heart feel like it was breaking from the longing for it.

He looked at his hand and then held it out toward her. Slowly, he uncurled his fingers.

Light glinted off of a dozen charms. Charms she recognized.

Hayley gasped and slid forward, barely managing to get to her feet and stay there. Her knees were so wobbly, she would probably fall any moment. She cupped her hand beneath his, unable to look away from the bracelet. The man tilted his hand, letting it fall into her palms.

Hayley let herself drop to her knees. She brought the charm bracelet to her face, tears flowing down her cheeks. Blinking them away, she looked at each one, remembered each year that she and Sophie had exchanged them. The last one was the half-heart BFF charm. Its edge was bent where Hayley had used it to try to pry open a panel back in the first cell she'd found herself in. The cell in the Sol system.

She looked back up at the blue man and shook her head. "How do you have this? Why are you here?"

"I don't know where it came from," he said. "I don't know who I am. All I know is that I'm here for you."

—

Rom's book is a bit more grim than the other stories, but don't worry! Nothing bad happens to the dog. The people? Well… They get a happy ending at least! But they will go through some stuff to get there. Be sure to watch for the last *Cygnian 7* book, *Rom: A Scifi Alien Warriors Romance* and complete your series!

If you want to learn more about Bron and the other Cygnian warriors' universe, you can check out *The Department of Homeworld Security* adventures. Many of the novellas have been collected in the first two series omnibuses, *The Department of Homeworld Security Omnibus 1* and *The Department of Homeworld Security Omnibus 2*. Or you can pick and choose with the individual novellas. You'll want to check out *Duration of Stay* to meet the Earthling who won Zemanni's heart and *Business or Pleasure* to see how Norem (aka 'Norm') began his evil schemes.

I'd love to keep in touch. Join my newsletter at cassandra-chandler.com to hear about all the adventures happening in Cassland. And if you enjoyed this book, please consider leaving a review at your favorite book review site. I'd really appreciate it—reviews help readers and authors alike!

Thank you for reading *Tarn: A Scifi Alien Warriors Romance!*

Cassandra Chandler

About the Author

USA Today Bestselling author Cassandra Chandler uses her vivid imagination to make the world more interesting, spawning the ideas she turns into her captivating Science Fiction Romances and enthralling Paranormal and Urban Fantasy Romances. Fast-paced and funny, lighthearted or filled with suspense, her stories will introduce you to characters you'll fall in love with and worlds you long to explore.